A MATTER OF PRIDE

Working for the opera star Bede Evans and his glamorous wife Jasmine is the perfect job for Rhianna O'Neill — until she inherits a wilful sixteen-year-old half sister after the tragic death of their mother in an accident . . . Then Rhianna's life is shattered by her broken engagement to Sax, Bede and Jasmine's son, and she takes off for France with handsome Luc Fermier, an old flame from her past. But that is when her problems really begin . . .

MARGARET MOUNSDON

A MATTER OF PRIDE

Complete and Unabridged

LINFORD
Leicester

First published in Great Britain in 2010

First Linford Edition
published 2011

British Library CIP Data

Mounsdon, Margaret.
    A matter of pride. - -
(Linford romance library)
1. Singers- -Fiction. 2. Women employees- -
Family relationships- -Fiction. 3. Mothers- -
Death- -Fiction. 4. France- -Fiction.
5. Love stories. 6. Large type books.
I. Title II. Series
823.9'2–dc22

ISBN 978–1–4448–0634–2

Published by
F. A. Thorpe (Publishing)
Anstey, Leicestershire

Set by Words & Graphics Ltd.
Anstey, Leicestershire
Printed and bound in Great Britain by
T. J. International Ltd., Padstow, Cornwall

This book is printed on acid-free paper

1

Rhianna's green eyes were clouded with unhappiness as they confronted those of Jasmine Evans over the breakfast table. Early April sun poured through the open conservatory door, cutting a swathe of light across the cork matting. In the distance the falls of Abercoed could be heard tumbling down the steep rock side into the mountain stream below.

Rhianna wanted to be outside, feeling the cool spray on her face, dipping her toes in the icy-cold water, smelling the spring air coming off the pine trees nestling in their narrow wooded gorge. She didn't want to be indoors struggling with yet another letter from Ayshea's headmistress.

Jasmine glanced up from reading her own letter, a sympathetic smile curling the corners of her mouth.

'Not more problems?' she queried.

How could anyone look so stunning this early in the morning in that shade of peacock-blue silk? thought Rhianna. *And after a late night too.* When Jasmine and Bede gave a party, they didn't do things by halves and last night had been no exception. It had been well into the small hours when they'd finally bid farewell to their guests.

'I'm not sure,' Rhianna admitted.

Jasmine glanced through the rest of her own letter. She blinked several times before placing it carefully on the table.

'The letter is from Miss Adams?' Jasmine inspected the envelope that lay on the table.

'Yes. It's about Ayshea.'

'I guessed that much.'

'Her mock exam results were poor.'

Jasmine poured out some squeezed orange juice and sipped it, then took a slice of wholemeal toast from the rack, spread it with honey and nibbled at a corner, before delicately patting the

2

crumbs off her lips.

Dancing beams of sunlight caught the ragged red highlights in Rhianna's hair as she pushed corkscrew tendrils away from her face. The curls immediately bounced back.

'Is that a problem?' Jasmine asked with a placid smile. 'I was never one for exams. Neither was Bede.'

Rhianna bit down a retort. Did nothing faze her glamorous employer?

Over the past six months, her life had lurched from one crisis to another — ever since that dreadful day when the police had knocked at the door of Bede's converted 17th century barn, tucked away in a remote village in North Wales on the edge of Snowdonia, to give her the dreadful news about the accident.

The sound of the daily starting up the vacuum cleaner brought Rhianna back to the present. She folded the letter into its envelope and picked up the rest of the day's post.

'I should get on. Itineraries don't sort

themselves out.'

Jasmine took another bite of toast. 'Let me know if I can be of any help.'

'You've done more than enough,' Rhianna said softly.

'Ayshea's coming up for the weekend, isn't she?'

'If that's all right with you?'

'Of course it is, darling. You don't have to ask.' Jasmine's almond eyes glowed with genuine pleasure. 'We love having her here. It's good to have young people about the place. They give off a happy karma.'

'Ayshea's not a very nice person at the moment.'

'We Orientals understand the grief process, Rhianna. Ayshea's full of anger right now. It will soften. Her world has been turned upside down, at the most vulnerable time of her life. Girls of sixteen need their mothers. She has lost hers, and her father. It may not seem like it at the moment, but it's important that you are there for her.'

'I'm not sure I can do anything for

her, Jasmine. We've never been close. Our relationship isn't easy.' Rhianna's eyes clouded again as she remembered Ayshea's numerous rebuffs of her attempts at friendship.

'These things take time.' Jasmine patted Rhianna's hand. 'Believe me. I went through it all with Sax. One day you'll find the sulky teenager has turned into a reasonable human being and you'll wonder how it happened. Now, are you sure you don't want any breakfast before you start work? It's important to keep up your strength.'

Rhianna took a slice of toast and buttered it, but after one mouthful she put it down on her plate, unable to eat any more. She hadn't had time to work through her own grieving process; Ayshea had seen to that. There was no one to whom she could turn. Kind though she was, Jasmine had her hands full looking after Bede. Rhianna had never felt so alone in her life.

Her mother Lesley, and Guy, her second husband, Rhianna's handsome stepfather . . . Rhianna shook her head. She couldn't believe she would never see them again. They had been on holiday in Amalfi and were driving home. The Italian police had said the accident was Guy's fault. Something about him forgetting to drive on the right after a sharp turn in the road.

Rhianna's throat locked. If it hadn't been for the generosity of Jasmine and Bede, Rhianna didn't know how she would have got through the dark days that followed.

Ayshea had been inconsolable, and aimed her aggression at Rhianna, who could do nothing to control her wilful half-sister's grief.

'I hate you!' she'd yelled at Rhianna as she tried to comfort the sobbing girl after the church service. 'Don't come near me. This is your fault.'

Irrational as her accusations were, they'd stabbed Rhianna to the heart. She wanted Ayshea to like, possibly even love, her. She wanted to have a sister she could love in return and be proud of. Instead, Ayshea had turned against her, rejecting her advances.

Ayshea's headmistress had accompanied her to the funeral and agreed it would be better if Ayshea went straight back to school.

'Her exams are coming up soon, Rhianna,' Miss Adams had said. 'Routine and focus are what Ayshea needs right now. If Mr and Mrs Evans are agreeable, she can spend occasional weekends with you. Ayshea's always been headstrong. Leave her with me and her friends. Given space and time, she'll come round.'

Rhianna had felt a guilty stab of relief at being rid of Ayshea as she'd driven away from the church. But her headmistress was right. The two sisters needed a break from each other. Ayshea would be happier with her classmates and Rhianna had more than enough to do, juggling personal and professional life, helping Bede with the arrangements for his tour, at the same time sorting through endless family legalities, without the anxiety of Ayshea's tantrums. The latest threat had been to walk out of school and not even sit her exams. No amount of reasoning seemed to work.

And charming as he was, Bede had more than his fair share of artistic temperament. In return for the generous salary he paid Rhianna, he expected minimal interruption to his hectic schedule. Rhianna couldn't walk out on him without giving notice, but neither could she abandon Ayshea, even though she was impossible to deal with at times.

If only Rhianna could talk to Sax. But he was in Germany. No one knew of their secret engagement, not even his beloved mother Jasmine.

'Not good for the image to have a fiancée, Babes.' He'd kissed her before leaving for his German tour eight weeks ago.

Since then she'd received one email and a rushed telephone call that had been interrupted by what sounded like a female voice in the background.

Sax was a party animal and Rhianna had learned to live with his lifestyle. That didn't stop her wondering if he was as committed to their engagement as she was. The lead singer in the band had told her it was usual for Sax to have several girlfriends on the go at the same time.

Rhianna had hoped things would gradually start to assume some sense or order, until this morning's mail and the latest letter from Miss Adams.

She left Jasmine watering her plants in the conservatory and walked through the open-plan day room with its stunning views of the valley, past the gleaming concert grand piano, to the elegant suite of offices Jasmine had designed in clean, minimalist lines.

Rhianna enjoyed the smooth elegance of her office and every morning it was a pleasure to start work. But today her thoughts were elsewhere, with Lesley and Ayshea, her mother and half-sister. They had been so alike, beautiful, blonde and full of life. Rhianna was the cuckoo in the nest. She took after her father; quieter, introvert, artistic.

It was her father, with his love of wild romance, who'd christened her Rhianna. Con O'Neill had lived on the west coast of Ireland and Rhianna had chosen to stay with him after he and Lesley had separated. Together they'd shared a happy existence until his death, when Rhianna had come to England to live with her mother and her new family.

It hadn't been an easy arrangement. Space had been cramped in the terraced house and eight-year-old Ayshea had been forced to share her bedroom with Rhianna. She'd made it clear that Rhianna was not welcome.

At the first opportunity Rhianna had escaped, and after a series of jobs had eventually come to work as personal assistant to the famous Welsh tenor Bede Evans and his stunning Asian wife Jasmine.

They were noted figures on the international scene and life with them was chaotic, but stimulating. Rhianna loved every moment of it. Contact with her family had been reduced to birthdays and Christmas and the occasional duty visit. Sometimes Ayshea had been at home, sometimes not. The age gap between them had meant few shared interests, resulting in the sisters growing up virtual strangers.

And over the last two years, Ayshea had changed so much that Rhianna hardly recognised her. Gone were the chubby face, crooked teeth and blonde plaits. Ayshea had shot up six inches and now sported a sleek bob. She had slender limbs, clear eyes and a freckle-free complexion Rhianna would have killed for.

Rhianna realised too, belatedly, that she'd not really known Lesley and Guy that well, either. They'd lived a day-to-day existence, Guy relying on family money to see him along.

It was only after their death that Rhianna also realised they didn't own their small terraced house and that the family money had long since been swallowed up by Guy's extravagant lifestyle. He was a man who liked to live well — foreign holidays, the latest model car every year with top of the range accessories, good restaurants, membership of the golf club.

Had it not been for a trust fund set up by her paternal grandfather, Ayshea would not have been able to stay on at her school, another issue to give Rhianna sleepless nights. What would happen if the money ran out?

Jasmine had been kindness itself, offering Ayshea a home at Abercoed for as long as she wished. For the moment Rhianna was grateful to accept Jasmine's offer as a temporary arrangement, but she knew she couldn't rely on her employer's hospitality forever.

The thought of giving up her job, to provide a home for a half-sister who didn't like her, seemed to be the only option.

And where would that leave Sax? Would he want Ayshea living with them when they got married? Sax was gregarious and selfish. Rhianna couldn't fool herself on that one. Looking after a teenage half-sister-in-law with attitude would not be his idea of married life.

Rhianna couldn't bear to think about it. Abercoed had been her life. She'd worked for Bede for four years and every day had been different, challenging, but always stimulating. And now it was all falling apart.

She sat down at her desk. Decisions would have to be made about Ayshea's future, and if she continued to fail her exams, Rhianna could foresee yet more problems.

In the quiet of her office Rhianna doodled on the pad of paper in front of her, a mermaid, with flowing hair and huge eyes. Her father had always referred to her hair as having the colour of rusty seaweed.

Guy Meredith, Ayshea's father, had been a kind man, but remote, very different from Con O'Neill. Guy always looked at Rhianna as if he wasn't quite sure what she was doing in his house.

Rhianna scored her pencil through her drawings. Daydreaming about mermaids and the past would get her nowhere. Like it or not, Ayshea was now her responsibility, and she'd never been one to shirk her duty. Infuriating though she was, difficult and demanding, Ayshea was still her sister. And sisters stuck together. Those were the rules. The sibling emotion was still there, even if it was buried deep under other stuff — dormant, but not extinct.

The house suddenly reverberated with the deep tones of Bede's voice as he began practising for his forthcoming tour. Last night's party had been a farewell bash for his friends and, as the routine of the house slowly returned to normal, Rhianna listened for a few moments. She never tired of the Italian operas and her heart soared with Bede's voice as he sung of Rodolfo's pain of unrequited love.

The last notes of his aria from *La Bohème* died away, leaving Rhianna emotionally refuelled. Reluctantly she picked up the telephone again and dialled Ayshea's school.

2

Several days later, Jasmine poked her head round the door of Rhianna's office. 'Sax will be home sometime this week.'

'Sax?' Rhianna repeated, not sure how she felt about seeing him again. After last weekend, she wasn't sure how she felt about anything.

'And with something special to tell us.' Jasmine raised a finger to her lips. 'I have been sworn to secrecy.' She had difficulty keeping the maternal pride out of her voice. 'He told me to make sure you're here, so no rushing off after that sister of yours.' Her eyes twinkled with pleasure as she watched Rhianna's blush deepen. 'I know how much you're looking forward to seeing him again.'

Rhianna hated being so pale-skinned. She always coloured up when she was happy, or annoyed, or sad, or for almost any emotional occasion. And the mention of Sax's name had her acting like a giddy schoolgirl, which at the age of twenty-two was absurd. She'd known Sax for years. It had been through him that she'd got this job. Charismatic and unconventional, he was always surrounded by a flock of people, mostly females.

'Do you want me to do anything? Make up beds? Go shopping?'

'That's very kind of you to ask, darling. I can manage. You've enough to do for Bede and Ayshea.'

'I'm sorry about last weekend, Jasmine.'

'You have nothing to apologise for.' Jasmine's plucked eyebrows met her fringe. 'Whatever gave you that idea?'

'Ayshea's behaviour was appalling. I was glad to see the back of her and I'm sure you must have been, too.'

Saturday's scene had left Rhianna drained and in need of a quiet walk. She'd taken the rocky path to the falls, welcoming the pain at the back of her legs as she'd climbed higher and higher, relishing the spray in her face as the water spritzed past her on its downward journey. She'd looked into the splashing coolness and wished she could plunge into its icy depths, cleanse away her troubles.

'I don't need you to tell me what I can and can't do, or how to run my life.' Ayshea had hurled the words at Rhianna as she'd tried to explain the importance of exam passes with good grades. 'I don't want to stay at school, anyway. It sucks.'

With that, she'd slammed doors and stomped off to her room. The next moment the barn had reverberated to the boom of her stereo. Rhianna had been grateful Bede had been away recording an interview. Roomy though the barn was, it wouldn't easily accommodate two fragile egos.

'What's a little loud music?' Jasmine said soothingly. 'I'm used to that, having Sax for a son and Bede for a husband. Why do you think we chose to live way up here?' Her sweet smile lit up her face. 'No neighbours to complain about the noise. As for Ayshea, she's still hurting.'

Jasmine's perfume lingered on the air after she closed the door. It was a special blend she had made up for her by one of the Parisian fashion houses — exotic, with a twist of mystery in its spicy base notes. A bit like the whole family, Rhianna thought as she inspected the latest booking arrangements Bede's agent had emailed through that morning. The schedule was tight and would require precise organisation.

Rhianna applied herself to the list and tried hard not to think about Ayshea, or Sax, who only had to play one note of his saxophone to have every female within earshot reduced to jelly.

Sax Pepper, of The Pepper Pots jazz band — apparently Bede had gone orbital when Sax had changed his name from Ewan and opted for jazz rather than classical, but Jasmine had been on her son's side and Bede had eventually been won round by his son's charm and undisputed talent.

Engrossed in her work, Rhianna didn't notice the time pass. She looked up with a start as papers flew across the desk, disturbed by Jasmine opening the door.

'Sorry,' Jasmine apologised. 'I've left you a light lunch, so make sure you eat it.'

'Lunch?' Rhianna frowned at her watch. 'It's only eleven o'clock.'

'Bede and I have to leave now for that TV interview. They've rescheduled. I don't know when we'll be back. You will be okay?'

'Of course.' Rhianna smiled. 'Have a good time.'

Jasmine made a face. 'Bede is being very trying. You know how artistic he gets before a tour.'

'For artistic, read wound up and driving everyone mad with the exception of his saintly wife?' Rhianna teased her employer.

Jasmine blew her a kiss. 'Don't forget

19

your lunch. I know what you're like. By the way, do you remember Luc Fermier?'

Rhianna felt a quick throb in her chest. How could she forget the Frenchman who had stolen her heart when she'd first come to work for Bede four years ago? She was too young then to realise that flirting with every female under the age of forty was a way of life for Frenchmen. It had meant nothing to Luc, but everything to Rhianna.

Luc was an old friend of Bede's and occasionally, in the summer, Bede and Jasmine would visit him if their schedules permitted.

'Luc Fermier? He's coming here?' Rhianna asked.

'It's been a while since we've seen him. He's had a few problems in his personal life and he's moving back to France from America. We're thinking of visiting him in the summer. If we're out when he arrives, can you entertain him for us?'

With a supreme effort Rhianna

managed to keep smiling as she waved at Jasmine from the window as the studio car taking her and Bede to their interview departed. Peace descended on the barn.

Rhianna had known that one day she would probably have to face Luc Fermier again. She still remembered the shock she'd felt when she took a telephone call from his wife.

Rhianna took a deep breath. She had grown up since those days, and she had other, more important things on her mind — such as a huge pile of paperwork to get through, easier to complete without interruptions. Much as she loved Jasmine, she could be a distraction, especially when she was planning her wardrobe for one of Bede's tours.

In the distance, the telephone rang. Rhianna picked up the latest email outlining yet another change in Bede's itinerary and ignored the telephone, letting the answering machine record the call.

Bede's European tour was due to start in a few days and it was vital she made no mistakes over the arrangements. She had to know exactly where he was, and when, in order for messages to be passed on. She ticked each detail as she entered it in the computer, then recorded it in a notebook, a fail-safe method she found worked best for her.

The telephone rang again. Rhianna worked steadily through the schedule. Eventually she completed the list, every item ticked and re-entered in her own personal diary of Bede's movements. It helped to have a simple book as a back-up. Memory sticks could be easily mislaid or corrupted, but her little notebook never attracted a virus. Transferring the tour details, however, always required an intense amount of concentration.

Satisfied with the accuracy of her work, Rhianna re-capped her pen. Anyone looking at the itinerary would know now to within a few hours exactly where Bede was and how to contact him. Should Rhianna be called away unexpectedly, or should one of Bede's numerous other assistants want to know details such as hotels or telephone numbers, it was all in Rhianna's little black book.

Her back ached and her eyes were gritty. Rhianna massaged her neck. Her stomach rumbled angrily. As usual, she'd lost all sense of time. She stood up slowly and stretched her aching limbs before making her way into the kitchen. Jasmine had laid out a tray for her on the breakfast bar. Rhianna poured spring water into a glass and sipped it slowly as she nibbled on a piece of bread and cheese.

Abercoed Barn was split-level, but every room, including the kitchen, had superb views. Full-length reinforced glass ensured an uninterrupted panorama. This afternoon the sky was a mixture of azure blue and puffball clouds of white.

Rhianna opened the top half of the

stable style back door and shivered in the cool breeze. Even in summer, the weather could be sharp.

Down in the valley she could see a slash of red as a car zigzagged round the bends, darting along like a dragon-fly. She loved this part of the world. It reminded her of the west-coast penin-sula of Ireland, rugged and romantic, but softer round the edges.

She finished her snack leaning over the door, revelling in the beauty and peace of the afternoon. Turning back into the kitchen, she flicked on the percolator, then sighed as the telephone began ringing again. If it was Jasmine and she could get no reply from the barn, she would worry.

Rhianna headed into the hall. The telephone stopped ringing before she reached it. The Messages Received light was flashing.

'Hi.' Sax's gravelly voice was its usual mixture of lightness and laughter. A smile softened Rhianna's lips as she listened. 'Landed safely. See you all soon. And have I got a surprise for you.' With kissing noises, he hung up.

Rhianna was still smiling as the next message clicked in. 'Rhianna?' The pencil fell from her fingers as she recognised the voice. 'Miss Adams here. It's half past two in the afternoon now. Ayshea did not return from lunch with the rest of her class after they went to visit the local business park. I've alerted the police.'

Rhianna snatched up the receiver and pressed the recall button. She didn't remember asking for the headmistress, but a few moments later she came on the line.

'Rhianna?' Her voice was breathless. 'Thank heavens you've called back. Is Ayshea with you?'

'With me? No, she isn't. What happened?' Rhianna demanded.

'I'm so sorry, Rhianna. The business park had an open day and a careers exhibition. It was only during the afternoon roll call that her housemistress realised Ayshea hadn't come back. One of the other girls had covered for her over the lunch period. The police are interviewing her roommate now. I've been worried something like this might happen. We've offered pastoral care, but she has always refused any help and we can't force it on her.'

Rhianna swayed and clutched the hall table for support. 'Have you any idea where she's gone? She's only sixteen.'

Rhianna thought of Ayshea's newly highlighted hair, a birthday treat, and the clothes Rhianna had bought her. She could look years older than sixteen. Her blood ran cold.

'One of her friends thinks she may be heading to Wales. It's not far.'

'To Abercoed? She's coming here?'

'She was upset over an argument you had at the weekend.'

The back of Rhianna's eyes grew hot as she remembered shouting back at Ayshea when she was at her most difficult. Harsh words had been exchanged. Rhianna hadn't meant any of it, but

Ayshea had been worse than impossible. Rhianna had been under pressure from Bede to get some last-minute press releases issued, and Ayshea's tantrum had been the final straw. And now Ayshea was missing, and it was all Rhianna's fault. She shouldn't have said what she had.

Rhianna pushed damp hair away from her face. What could she do? She couldn't go looking for Ayshea and leave the barn unoccupied, even in an emergency. Bede was paranoid about security. His collection of memorabilia, recordings, photographs, documents, were all stored in the safe, but he didn't trust security systems and insisted either Jasmine or Rhianna remain at the barn at all times.

'Are her things missing?'

'Her bag and some money. That's all.'

A noise on the terrace distracted Rhianna. She turned. A shadow was inching towards the back door. A scream caught in Rhianna's throat. Had she locked up before coming to answer the phone? She couldn't remember.

The receiver fell from her fingers. She strained her ears. There was no mistaking the sound of soft footsteps on the patio. Someone was outside. And Rhianna was alone in The Barn. The village of Abercoed was over a mile away, down the dusty road past where she'd seen the flashing red car. She glanced at the list of numbers Jasmine kept by the telephone in case of emergency, but they were of the doctor, dentist variety. Even the local police wouldn't be able to get up the winding hill road in time to help her.

Her limbs froze as she heard hushed voices. She lunged at the door in an attempt to lock it. Her action was greeted with a shriek of surprise.

'Rhianna! It's me.'

'Ayshea! You're safe.' Rhianna sobbed and hugged her sister so hard that she almost cracked her ribs. She kissed the fragrant hair as her tears and words got caught up together. 'Miss Adams said you'd run away.'

She stroked Ayshea's hair, deciding that if this was what it felt like to be a mother she wasn't sure she wanted any children.

'Rhianna, I'm sorry.' Ayshea's voice was a muffled moan.

Rhianna's relief at knowing nothing had happened to her beautiful, wayward sister released the stopcock on her emotions.

'Don't ever do anything like that again.'

'I didn't think. I'm really sorry, Rhianna.'

'If I lost you too, I don't know what I would do.'

The blue eyes facing hers were drowning in tears. 'Do you mean that?'

'Of course I mean it.'

'Then don't be cross with me,' Ayshea pleaded. 'I only wanted to apologise for being so horrid to you. I feel so chewed up about the wrecked weekend, about the way I behaved to you and Jasmine.'

Rhianna's heart softened. She'd never

been very good at being angry and Ayshea was so beautiful that it was impossible to be cross with her for long. But the girl needed to be taught a lesson.

'So you should be. You'll have to apologise to Jasmine and Bede.'

A tiny tear trickled down Ayshea's surprisingly dirty face. Her hair, too, Rhianna noted, now she'd run out of steam and paused to look properly at her sister, was unkempt and stuck wetly to her head. Rhianna bit her lip.

Her eyes fell to the grubby T-shirt and oil-stained cargo pants. The core of Rhianna's anger melted briefly, before she remembered that Ayshea was a professional at dewy-eyed repentance. She'd seen her work the stunt on Guy and Lesley many times.

'I'm really, really sorry, Rhianna.'

'Prove it. Get on that telephone. *Now*,' Rhianna pointed to the table with military discipline, 'and call Miss Adams. Explain what you've done and assure your headmistress you're safe. If you're lucky the police may not press charges.' Rhianna wasn't sure about that, but she decided Ayshea could take a few more shocks. She was tougher than she looked. 'Then we'll talk. Now,' Rhianna repeated as Ayshea glanced over her shoulder.

'I hate to interrupt things,' a male voice drawled from the doorway.

Rhianna froze to the spot.

'Rhianna,' Ayshea hissed, 'this is . . . '

'I know who this is.' Rhianna hoped she sounded cool and in control.

'He gave me a lift from the village.'

The man moved away from the kitchen door and into the hall. Rhianna hadn't remembered him being quite so tall. He was wearing a polo shirt of deep blue, but it didn't disguise the powerful muscles of his arms.

'Hello. Luc Fermier, isn't it?' Rhianna did her best to sound casual.

'Rhianna.' His voice still had the power to make her spine tingle. 'It's good to see you again — you've changed, and for the better.'

Rhianna tossed back her hair. She

was no longer the silly girl she had once been, who fell for his smooth charm. She didn't return the compliment.

'Please,' Luc pleaded, 'I have a request. Don't be too hard on Ayshea.'

'Perhaps you'd leave family matters to me. Thank you.' Rhianna could feel anger curling up again in her stomach. 'You don't know my sister, but let me tell you, she can work any situation to her advantage, especially if there's a member of the opposite sex involved.'

'I'm sure what you say is absolutely true.'

'And at the risk of being impolite, Mr Fermier . . . '

'Luc, please.'

'Very well, Luc, the situation between my sister and me has nothing to do with you.'

The next moment, three things happened. Ayshea got through to Miss Adams, and began apologising down the telephone.

Then Sax strolled in. 'Anyone in? Been hammering on the door for what seems like hours.'

A second later, an extremely thin girl with ravishing burnished copper hair appeared in the doorway.

'Hello.' With a friendly smile she held out a hand. Her poncho top couldn't disguise the fact she was pregnant. 'I'm Sax's wife.'

3

Rhianna pushed her hair away from her face as the breeze, with its peculiar mixture of scents of hazel and lime, stroked her neck.

'*Bonjour, mam'zelle.*'

She smiled an acknowledgement to the dignified gentleman who pushed his bicycle past her as she sat in the cobblestone square, listening to the gentle trickle of the central fountain. It soothed her jangled nerves, which were still in trauma over recent events.

Accompanying Luc Fermier to France was a disastrous idea and if Rhianna hadn't been so stunned by Sax's appearance with Heidi, she'd have been able to think up a good enough excuse to convince Jasmine why she should not go.

It was the only time in her life Rhianna had ever seen Jasmine lose her cool. She'd known about Sax's marriage from the letter he'd sent her, but he'd asked his mother not to tell Rhianna. Her joy over his news had turned to anger when she'd found out about their secret engagement.

'You mean you had an understanding with Rhianna?' she'd hissed at her son, finding the pair of them arguing in the kitchen at two in the morning.

Rhianna had been unable to sleep. Hearing her moving about, Sax had followed her downstairs and tried to explain how he'd thought he loved her until he met Heidi.

'Jasmine, please,' Rhianna implored, anxious now to get back to bed and forget the day had ever occurred. 'It's late. We've got a busy day tomorrow — I mean today.'

'How could you do this?'

'I don't know,' Sax confessed. 'It happened. And I do love Heidi. You understand, Rhianna, don't you? It was never official between us, anyway.'

Rhianna had had to harden her heart, not to smile back at Sax. He may not have thought their arrangement was official — but she had.

Even now, she couldn't believe it. Sax was married, to a beautiful German girl. Rhianna's pride had not let Sax see how his actions hurt her.

The spring sun was warm on Rhianna's back and she wished she'd been brave enough to wear her shorts, but her pale flesh wasn't ready for the full force of the French midday sun. She pulled off her long-sleeved cotton jumper and folded it in her lap.

With as much dignity as she could muster, she'd returned Sax's gold locket containing their two photographs. They'd chosen it together as a symbol of their love, instead of an engagement ring. Rhianna's neck felt bare without it.

And now, here she was in France with Luc Fermier, on the pretence of arranging a charity appearance for Bede at the Fête du Chanson once his tour was over. Bede was a man of healthy appetites and after the strict regime of a tour, he liked to unwind with good food, fine wine, sunshine and pleasant company. That was why Jasmine had made arrangements for Luc Fermier to contact them, and why she had insisted Luc and Rhianna travelled back to France together at the first opportunity.

'You need space away from Sax, Ayshea and Bede,' Jasmine insisted. 'Staying with Luc in Haut Roque will provide the distraction you need.'

'What about his wife?' Rhianna demanded.

'He's not married,' Jasmine replied.

Drained of emotion, Rhianna lacked the will to argue with her. There had been time for only a few snatched words with Luc, who seemed to have no objection to the arrangement, and before Rhianna could protest further the bookings were made.

'Shall we go?' Luc emerged from the café, having settled their lunch bill.

Not for the first time, Rhianna wondered how her taste in men could be so disastrous. First Luc, now Sax

— both had let her down badly.

'I wish you'd let me contribute to our expenses.' Rhianna stood up.

'It is my pleasure,' Luc insisted, his eyes searching her pale face. He nodded, noting she had taken off her cotton top. 'See, the sun is already doing you good.'

'Thank you, but I'm used to paying my own way.'

Luc jangled his car keys with a Gallic gesture of irritation. 'I haven't time to argue if we're to get to Haut Roque before nightfall. We can talk later.'

His English was fluent, but when he spoke quickly, there was still a trace of an accent.

'I'm not arguing,' Rhianna insisted.

'*Bon*. Then we'll be on our way.'

Luc strode towards his sleek red open-topped Aston, the one Rhianna had seen darting up the mountain road five days earlier.

Left with no choice but to follow, she hurried after him as he held open the passenger door with an air of impatience. It had been like this all the way from the ferry.

Rhianna had felt like a washed-out rag after Jasmine had taken care of everything. Luc had driven a subdued Ayshea back to school after the weekend, while Heidi, with the help of Rhianna's copious notes, had been appointed Bede's temporary personal assistant.

'Think of it as a working holiday, darling.' Jasmine had kissed Rhianna goodbye. 'Bede and I will join you when the tour is over.'

'But I can't leave you in the lurch at the beginning of the tour.'

'Nonsense, we'll manage, and it's been ages since you've had a break. You're looking tired and pale. What you need is sunshine and some good food. Luc will look after you and it's not as if you're complete strangers.'

One glance at the way Sax had looked at his new wife, tenderly placing a cushion behind her back at the breakfast table, was enough for Rhianna. There was no place for her at Abercoed and, like it or not, Luc Fermier was her only escape option.

'And we will look after Ayshea for you,' Jasmine added.

Rhianna fastened her seatbelt as Luc reversed out of the parking bay. Every so often Rhianna glanced at his profile, noting the firm jawline, the high aristocratic cheekbones and lopsided smile which, like the breeze, was beginning to weave a calming kind of magic over her, a magic she didn't need, a magic she didn't want to understand.

She was battered and bruised and she wanted to hurt. She wanted to feel the full force of Sax's treachery. But Luc wouldn't let her. They argued, ate and laughed together. That had surprised Rhianna. She hadn't felt like laughing, but Luc was a good companion and knew how to be entertaining. He made no reference to their past, and as Rhianna began to relax in his company, she found it difficult to believe he had once been so dismissive of her attempts to seduce him.

'Comfortable?' he asked. Reaching the main road, he put his foot down.

'Thank you. Yes.'

The wind whipped Rhianna's hair into a frenzy of curls that refused to behave. Her complexion was beginning to react to the sun and fresh air. She suspected her appearance was beginning to resemble that of a shaggy dog, far removed from the chic French females they passed as they drove along the tree-lined roads on their way to the Dordogne.

Luc had chosen the scenic route through rolling countryside, fields dotted with huge ox-eye daisies, cool forests, and tiny villages where geese seemed to hold the *droit de seigneur* for walking across roads.

Now the landscape was changing into wooded hills and winding valleys with spectacular views of the limestone plateaus.

'I am *Périgourdin*,' Luc had informed her over lunch as they'd torn chunks of fresh bread from a huge loaf, dipping it into garlic butter, before it melted over crevettes that were bigger even than the Dublin Bay prawns Rhianna and her father used to enjoy. 'The area is famous for its patés and truffles, and wine of course.'

Rhianna sipped a glass of fresh orange and tried to make a civilised attempt at conversation. Luc had suggested wine, but lunchtime drinking was something Rhianna wasn't ready for, even though she was in France.

'I always want to fall asleep in the afternoon if I drink at lunchtime.'

'The English,' Luc teased her, 'need to relax more.'

Rhianna refused to rise to his bait. There was something about arguing with Luc that excited her. He was different from Sax, and still so very attractive. She knew she was on dangerous ground if she did anything to inflame the tension she was feeling every time he looked at her, and she had absolutely no intention of making a fool of herself for a second time.

'Actually,' he said, 'I should not tease you. I am half English too.'

Rhianna stared at him in surprise.

'You did not know? My father was English, but my French grandparents brought me up. They were proud people who worked hard and expected their daughter to marry someone local. It was a great culture shock to them when my mother began going out with an Englishman, a man they knew nothing about. His lifestyle was different from theirs. They were country people, who worked the land. My father was,' Luc shrugged, 'something of a *boulevardier*. Then when my mother fell pregnant,' Luc paused, 'it sounds old-fashioned now, but the shame was almost too much for her parents to bear. They were the targets of local gossip. Haut Roque is the sort of place where everyone knows everyone. You have places like this in England too?'

'And Ireland,' Rhianna agreed.

'His eyes strayed to her unruly red hair. 'You are Irish? That explains the Celtic temperament, fizzy like a firework.'

Rhianna shifted uncomfortably in her seat. Luc was teasing her. She could tell by his eyes. They changed colour when he was amused.

'I'm half-English too, like you,' she retaliated.

'A good mix, non? The romanticism of France and mystique of Ireland.'

'What about the English bit?'

'You have a little bit of that too, practical, loyal and — ' Luc paused.

'And what?'

'A soft heart.'

Rhianna had swallowed the last of her fruit juice almost too quickly. She swallowed down a cough, unsure why she was finding it so difficult to breathe. The way Luc was talking, looking at her, was so very different from how it had been with Sax. Sax always had to be the centre of attention. When he wasn't, he sulked. Sax was high-maintenance, but Luc seemed to care what Rhianna thought and how she felt.

'Do you have a soft heart, too?' she challenged.

Luc's mouth twisted into its lopsided smile. 'I think I must have, a bit. Why else would I have landed myself with a female who reminds me of a rocket and Catherine Wheel all rolled into one? You were like a firecracker with Ayshea — one big, colourful explosion.'

'We were talking about your family,' Rhianna reminded him, feeling rather like a schoolteacher disciplining a cheeky child.

'So we were.' Luc leaned back in his chair and smiled. 'Are you sure you won't have any of this rosé? It really is very good. As you wish.' He poured himself a small glass. 'My parents' marriage did not last.'

Luc cut a slice of runny Brie and helped himself to some black grapes. Fascinated, Rhianna watched his fingers separate them from the cluster.

'Then after my mother died, my grandparents raised me. Gradually my memory of my father faded. He returned to England and I stayed here. There were occasional letters, photos were exchanged and birthday cards, but no visits. Eventually I lost touch with him.'

'That is very sad.'

Luc shrugged. 'It is life.' He dropped his grapes onto the plate. 'So now it's your turn.' He picked up a grape. 'I did not know you had a sister.'

A huge bowl of fresh peaches had been placed on the table, together with a wooden platter of walnuts.

'My parents, too, split up when I was young. I stayed in Ireland. I was fourteen when my father died and I came to England and lived with my mother and her new husband. I moved to London after college, met Sax and came to work for Bede Evans. The rest you know.'

'I hope he will be able to entertain us at our concert in the summer. Although

I appreciate Haut Roque isn't quite in his usual league,' Luc added with a rueful smile.

'That wouldn't worry Bede. He loves to sing anywhere in the world. To him it's all the same, whether it's in a local park, or the big opera houses.'

'You're very lucky to work for him.'

'It is — ' Rhianna paused — '*was* a wonderful job.'

Luc looked sympathetic. 'Tell me about Sax.'

'We met in a London nightclub. I worked there some evenings, taking the coats, that sort of thing, to make extra money. When it was quiet we used to talk. I wanted to leave London and Sax mentioned his father was looking for a new assistant. Jasmine came to town for a visit and Sax introduced me to his mother. We clicked straight away. In Bede's book, there's no better recommendation than to win his wife's approval.'

Rhianna could feel her throat getting hot again. Despite everything he'd done to her, there was still a part of Rhianna that would forever belong to Sax. The Bohemian-style suppers they'd shared after his performances at the clubs . . . the riotous parties with the group that had gone on until all hours . . . the lazy Sunday walks by the river, followed by pub lunches.

'And he never mentioned this Heidi to you?'

'No.' Rhianna snatched at a peach. Her appetite had deserted her, but she needed to do something with her hands before Luc had chance to notice they were trembling.

'I see.'

'No, you don't see at all.' Rhianna didn't want to discuss Sax but once she started, she found it difficult to stop.

'Sax is a party person. I've always known that. His parents are social people. Sax takes after them. He'd been in Germany for months. I was going for a visit, but I couldn't leave Ayshea. Her state of mind was too fragile and I feared she'd do something silly if she thought I'd deserted her.'

A spray of peach juice stained the checked tablecloth as Rhianna dug her fingers into its ripe softness. Rhianna licked the moisture from her fingers, missing the expression in Luc's eyes.

'Did you love Sax?'

'Of course I did.'

'Or did you love the idea of being in love?'

'What sort of a question is that?' Rhianna demanded, her fingers digging deeper into the velvet flesh of her peach. Was Luc referring to their past? Had she thought she was in love with Luc Fermier, too?

'A question that seems to unnerve you,' he answered gently. 'Would you like me to help you with that peach?'

'I can manage,' she snapped.

'Think of the poor peach,' he protested. 'You're killing it.'

Rhianna forced herself to swallow a slice. Its juice slipped down her throat, easing its soreness.

'It's delicious.'

'Peaches and walnuts are local specialities. In the old days Périgord food, the wine, cheeses and pâtés were food fit for kings. Did you know you have juice running down your chin?' Luc asked amusedly.

Rhianna wiped the drips away with the back of her hand and a shamefaced smile. 'Sorry, I do seem to be getting in a bit of a mess.'

'You should smile more often. It makes your eyes dance.'

'Well, I haven't exactly had much to smile about recently, have I?'

'Haut Roque will change all that.'

'Luc, I'm not at all sure I should have agreed to this trip. It's always a stressful time before Bede goes on tour. Heidi may not be able to handle it.'

'Jasmine tells me you left pages of notes and a comprehensive schedule. Heidi and Sax will have no difficulty following them while you're away. It's better you left them alone to get used to the situation. It probably wouldn't have been fair on Heidi if you had stayed, and the whole thing has been a shock for Jasmine and Bede too.'

'I should ring Jasmine.'

'I already have. She's fine and sends her love. Ayshea's behaving herself at school and Bede has had his first row with Heidi, so nothing wrong there.'

'I miss them.' Despite the soothing peach juice Rhianna's voice felt as rough as the walnut shells littering the table.

Luc placed a hand over hers. 'Once we arrive in Haut Roque you won't have time to miss them. Remember you are here to work. You have to charm the organisers into changing their itinerary for the Fête du Chanson. I know Bede Evans will be a great draw, but some of the committee are very stubborn. They resent outside interference. Things have been done a certain way since the days of Louis Quatorze and they don't see any reason for change. You're going to have your hands full persuading them.'

'Do you live alone?' Rhianna asked suddenly.

'Yes.' There was a pause. I have done, ever since my divorce. My wife was American. She found France not to her liking.' Luc frowned as he spoke. 'Now, if you are finished, we should press on.'

Rhianna's head was buzzing as Luc's car ate up the final miles of their journey. She should have enquired about the accommodation arrangements in Haut Roque, but everything had been arranged in such a rush she hadn't had time to think about the finer details of their trip. The thought of sleeping under the same roof as Luc was unnerving, and in normal circumstances a situation she would never have agreed to.

'The River Dordogne is one of the longest in France,' Luc informed her as they drove along. 'Haut Roque is one of the many hamlets situated along its banks. There is a 12th Century church, an auberge and a château on a high rock dominating the village. That's how it got its name. Years ago it was owned by a younger son of one of the big wine-growing families in the region. My grandparents lived in the coach house at the gate, seeing to his visitors and everyone's day-to-day needs. The owner died without ever having been married and he had no heirs. My grandparents discovered he'd bequeathed them the lodge in his will as repayment for their loyal service.'

'Is that, er, where we will be staying?' Rhianna asked delicately.

'It is. Wait until you see it. At this time of year the meadows are full of wild roses and poppies. The weather is starting to warm up and the days are longer. There are plenty of outdoor activities, too. Do you play boules?'

Rhianna shook her head. 'Isn't that a game played by very old men wearing straw hats?'

'Not at all. We have a local team, doing well in the league. One evening we will go and watch them play if you like.'

'Have you always lived in Haut Roque?'

'On and off. I have a studio in Paris and I did have a condo in New York, but I want to spend more time here in the future. The château and rest of the grounds have been sold off privately to a consortium that arranges conferences, that sort of thing, but I still have the lodge.'

'What did you do in America?'

'I ran my own international consultancy and I still intend to do so, but my roots are in France. With the breakdown of my marriage, it seemed a suitable time to move back.'

They'd left the main road now and were driving down country lanes alongside a meandering river, through picturesque villages, past rubble that had once, Luc told her, been castles.

'This area has a lot of history. The Dordogne was almost Europe's busiest waterway, and we have prehistoric caves and grottos. There's a lot to see during your stay. If you like, we can go up to the plateau. There's a local cable car that runs trips.'

Rhianna had never seen anything as colourful as the flowers in the meadows. The scenery in Ireland was beautiful, but wild. Here the hills and meadows were gentler and softer. The smells were so different from the sharp tangs of her childhood. She closed her eyes and felt Luc change gear beside her.

'Nearly there.' He made a left turn and the car began to climb carefully. Rhianna caught her breath at the views. Sunlight filtered through the trees, sparkling on the rooftops below. Without warning Luc swung through an ancient pair of narrow iron gates and drove a little way down a bumpy drive.

Nestling on the edge of a wood stood a small white lodge house, octagonal in shape, with a terracotta-coloured roof and diamond-paned windows. It reminded Rhianna of the fairytales she and her father used to read when she was a child.

'Welcome to *Le Pavillon de Jardin*.' Luc smiled at her. 'I think that's a summerhouse in English, isn't it?'

'Yes, it is.' Rhianna stared at it, entranced.

'My grandparents renamed it after they inherited it.'

A smile stretched Rhianna's face for the first time in days. She turned to look at Luc. 'It's beautiful. Thank you for inviting me.'

His answering smile caused her heart to flutter in her chest. She turned swiftly away, not wanting him to read the reaction in her eyes. Behind her she heard Luc close the car door and begin looking for his keys, normal everyday noises that helped to calm the turmoil raging inside her.

4

'Ayshea?' Rhianna's heart began its treble tattoo at the sound of her sister's voice on the telephone. 'What's wrong?'

'Nothing's wrong.' Ayshea's laughter bubbled down the line. 'I'm not in any trouble.'

'That makes a change.' Rhianna tried to sound frosty, but it didn't work very well. She was pleased to hear Ayshea's voice, and relieved all was well.

'I rang to see if you arrived safely. Luc gave me the number of the lodge before you left.'

Through the open window, Rhianna could see a brightly coloured bird darting across the dew-specked grass. She inhaled the fresh morning air. There was a mossy smell from the woods at the back of the house. They looked cool and inviting.

'Rhianna?'

'Yes?' Her fingertips tingled. Her Irish sixth sense was telling her this wasn't only a courtesy call.

'I'm sorry,' Ayshea mumbled down the line.

'What was that?' Rhianna forgot all about the kingfisher-coloured bird.

'I said I'm sorry,' Ayshea repeated in a rush. 'About me, about Sax, about everything. I wondered if we could start afresh. No, don't interrupt,' Ayshea carried on, her voice quickened by panic, 'it took ages to pluck up the courage to do this. Let me get it over in one go. If you still feel you want to, you can read me the riot act afterwards, although I've had the lecture several times from you, Miss Adams, Jasmine — even Luc had a go at me on the drive back to school. I mean, what business is it of his what I get up to?'

Ayshea's call had interrupted Rhianna's late and lazy breakfast after the best night's sleep she'd had for months, in a tiny bedroom under the eaves. Any fears she'd had about spending a night under the same roof as Luc had soon evaporated as, after sharing a scratch supper, he'd retreated to his study to catch up on emails.

'I like to work late,' he'd explained matter-of-factly. 'I'll see you in the morning. Sleep well.'

Someone had placed a lavender sachet on her pillow and Rhianna had fallen into a deep sleep as her head touched the clean, crisp bed linen. Nine hours later, she'd woken, struggling to remember where she was and why she was feeing so refreshed. But now she could feel the benefit of a good night's sleep already slipping away.

'You had words with Luc?' Rhianna repeated.

'Never mind him.' Ayshea dismissed the mention of his name. 'I've been awful to you, I know,' she rattled on, 'and to Jasmine too, so I've decided to go for the full dump therapy.'

Rhianna could hear her taking a deep breath. 'So I telephoned Jasmine in Italy to apologise for my behaviour and she said it was all right with her. She was so sweet. She said I was welcome back at Abercoed any time I liked. I couldn't talk for long because Bede was bellowing in the background for something or other. I could hear him.'

Rhianna ignored the stab of homesickness she felt for Jasmine and Bede and turned her attention back to what Ayshea was saying.

'Ayshea, what is this all really about? What is all right with Jasmine?' Experience had taught Rhianna that where Ayshea was concerned, it was best to be suspicious.

'Haven't you been listening to a word I've said?' Ayshea demanded. Sorry,' she backtracked, arousing Rhianna's further suspicions. Ayshea did not do apologising, especially not to Rhianna, and she became more than ever convinced that Ayshea was after something.

'I know I'm rabbiting on. It's nerves. I was just so devastated by what happened to Mummy and Daddy. I totally freaked. Mummy was always praising you to the skies, telling me what a wonderful example of an older sister you were. There were days when I had it to the teeth.

'Then when you didn't, well, show any emotion — you know, crack up or anything like that after the accident, I couldn't hack it. I cracked up for the both of us. That's the best way I can put it. You were the only one I could turn to so I took it out on you. I'm not making excuses, Sis, just telling it how it is. There. Finished. 'Cept I wanted you to know I'm really, really sorry.

'Hello?' Ayshea asked in a little voice after a pause, 'are you still there?'

'That was some dump therapy.' Rhianna struggled to speak. 'Why didn't you tell me this earlier?'

'I was scared to. You carried on like there was nothing wrong. I talked it through with my roommate at school, the one who covered for me that day after the visit to the business park? Anyway, we decided I had to say sorry to you personally. But the whole thing was a disaster, wasn't it? I didn't know Luc was going to turn up out of the blue, or Sax with a pregnant German wife.' Ayshea stumbled to a stop. 'Sorry. That was insensitive.'

'Yes, it was,' Rhianna admitted, wondering why Ayshea's words about Sax didn't hurt as much as usual.

'You've had a tough time too, haven't you? I know I'm not much good in a crisis, but if you need a shoulder to cry on, there's one available here.'

'Ayshea.' The back of Rhianna's throat felt tight. This was what being a sister was all about. Ayshea was the most infuriating, selfish, headstrong, beautiful creature she'd ever met. And Rhianna was at last beginning to realise she loved her to bits.

'Everything's all right then, between us?' Ayshea demanded anxiously.

'For the time being.' Rhianna held back a little. It was too soon to go soft on Ayshea. 'There's still some work to do in our relationship. Are you sure you've apologised to everyone you inconvenienced with your escapade?'

'Everyone, and if it's any consolation I was gated by Miss Adams when I got back.' Ayshea was back to being indignant again. 'Can you believe it?'

Rhianna struggled to keep the amusement from her voice. 'So, how are the exams going?'

'Sat the last one today. Economics. Yuk. My favourite subject — not. Still, that's it now. I'm not going to think about results.'

'When do you break up?'

'That's what I've been trying to tell you. I don't want to stay at Abercoed Barn with Heidi and Sax. I still think he's a rat for what he did to you and I might be persuaded to tell him so. Anyway, my roommate is coming down your way with her parents the day after tomorrow. They've taken a villa in the south of France. Can I come down with her? I've cleared it with Jasmine. You could pick me up, maybe. I know it's a bit short notice, but I mean, you're vulnerable at the moment, aren't you? I bet you don't want to be left alone with a sexy Frenchman do you? I could be your chaperone.'

A rueful smile twisted Rhianna's lips. At times, her young half-sister was way too observant, but it wouldn't do to agree with her. 'So that's what this call is about, is it?'

'Miss Adams says I need to improve my French if I want to be an air stewardess,' Ayshea wheedled.

'Who are these people offering you a lift?' Rhianna asked. 'Give me their details. I need to check a few things through, then I'll get back to you.'

'Thanks, Rhianna. You're the best sister in the world. I can't wait to see you again. What's it like down there?'

'Well, it's . . . '

'Hey, gotta go. This call is costing a fortune. I'm in Miss Adams' study. She said I could ring you, but I don't think she realised you're in France. Please, please say I can come?'

'If everything checks out, then yes.'

The jubilant screech that came down the line nearly deafened Rhianna as she rang off.

'Good morning.' Luc wandered onto the terrace, wearing a pale blue shirt and darker chinos. 'Who was that?' He poured himself juice and took a warm croissant from under the white linen serviette in the breadbasket.

He smelled of lime shower gel, clean and sharp. Rhianna had never liked the spicy smell of Sax's aftershave. It used to give her a headache. She realised with a start that she hadn't thought about Sax this morning until Ayshea had mentioned his name.

'It was Ayshea,' she replied to Luc's query.

Luc's buttered croissant hovered in mid-air. 'Now what's happened?'

Rhianna wanted to laugh at the expression on his face. She imagined it was how she must have looked so many times over the past few months every time her sister's name was mentioned.

'She doesn't fancy staying in Aber-coed with Heidi and Sax and she wants to come over here, the day after tomorrow. Her exams are finished and some friends are driving down.'

'Who are these friends?'

'I've said I'll check them out. If it's all right with you, can she come? I've sort of promised she can.'

'It'll mean a lot of work for you. One of the local women has been keeping the place tidy but she only comes in for an hour a day. I imagine Ayshea isn't the tidiest of creatures.'

'I don't mind, and I'll make sure she keeps her room tidy.'

Luc offered her coffee. Rhianna noticed that he drank his black and without sugar.

'Are you sure you're ready for her? I mean, this was supposed to be a break for you and Ayshea will want transport here, there and everywhere. And once the local lads discover there's a very attractive English girl staying we won't get any peace.'

Rhianna nodded. 'I'd like her to come. She sounded eager to see me

— us,' Rhianna amended.

Luc raised his eyebrows. 'Has she had a makeover?'

'I wouldn't go as far as that,' Rhianna admitted.

'In that case, I suggest we make the most of what could be one of our last free days together. I was going to suggest a trip out today to the grottoes.' Luc glanced at his watch. 'How about you make a list of everything you need while I do my telephone calls? We can visit the market in the old quarter first, then if we have time, take in a few of the sights.'

★   ★   ★

Haut Roque was too small to boast an old quarter, but the adjoining market town of St Cécile was a bustling place with antiquated houses and tiny back streets that were pedestrianised on market days, when rows of striped awnings were raised above street stalls groaning under the weight of fresh produce.

Rhianna had been to markets before, of course, but never one like this, with such a variety of smells and noises. Her halting attempts at shopping in French were greeted with helpful encouragement — and laughter, when she asked for a kilo of cabbages instead of Brussels sprouts.

'I can do it,' she'd insisted, when Luc had offered to help.

'As you wish,' he'd said, then crossed his arms and watched her struggle with her schoolgirl French. Pride wouldn't let her admit she'd wanted fresh lemons, as an enormous bag was filled to the brim with oranges and passed over to her. It split as Rhianna, rather red in the face, tipped them into her shopping bag.

'Do we need all this stuff?' Luc grumbled at another stall as Rhianna loaded yet another carrier bag with fruit and vegetables.

'Ayshea doesn't eat meat, and she has a healthy appetite.'

'I'd noticed.' Luc grimaced as he

picked it up. 'Have we finished?' he asked hopefully.

'What about some flowers for her room? Is that lavender? Look at the size of that garlic.' Distracted, Rhianna flitted backwards and forwards.

Luc groaned, wine bottles clanking against his legs as he tried to keep up with her. Rhianna darted over to a florist's stall.

'That is it,' he said firmly, 'shopping is over for the day.'

Rhianna thrust a bunch of luscious hydrangeas at him.

'Aren't they beautiful? I've never seen such deep blue.'

'Lovely. Now, are we finished? It's four o'clock in the afternoon, and a Frenchman does not like to be deprived of his lunch.'

Rhianna raised a horrified hand to her face. 'Is it that late? We won't be able to do the grottoes now, will we?'

'What a pity,' Luc said, not sounding too disappointed. 'I suggest we take this lot back to the car and then get something to drink. There's no need to panic. I'm not suggesting wine. Right now, I'm so dry I'd even drink a cup of your English coffee. That shows you how desperate I am.'

Laughing, Rhianna followed him across the cobbled square to the car. Traders were already beginning to dismantle their stalls.

'Have we got room for some of those?' Rhianna began as bunches of grapes at bargain prices were pressed on her by stallholders anxious to offload the last of their stock.

'No, we haven't.' Luc staggered to the car. 'How the blazes we're going to get this stuff in, I don't know. Hold that.'

Rhianna did as she was told. 'Did we really buy all this?' she asked.

'You did.' Luc's voice came from the depths of the boot as he thrust carriers this way and that. 'How can one extra person make for so much shopping?'

'I told you. Ayshea likes to eat well.'

'Does she eat fish?' Luc asked.

'Yes.'

'Good. Perhaps we can fill her up on that.' There was a cracking noise, followed by a muffled French curse. Luc straightened up and held out two broken halves of a baguette.

'You've got bits of hydrangea and breadcrumbs all over you.' Rhianna stood on tiptoe, biting down her amusement. Luc didn't look as though he could see the funny side of the situation. 'Here, let me.'

She picked mauve blossoms and bits of bread from his hair, trying hard not to look into his eyes, or notice how close her body was to his. She averted her eyes and caught sight of a boutique window filled with striped tops and white cropped trousers. A jaunty wide-brimmed sun hat had been placed at an angle on the model's head as she sat in a rowing boat, surrounded by fishing nets and crab shells.

Rhianna felt hot, grubby and unfashionable in her dowdy jeans and chain store T-shirt. The squashy contents of the shopping bag she had been clutching to her chest had seeped onto her top, leaving a smelly, colourful stain. Crushing the hydrangea blossom from Luc's hair in her hand, she watched the colour seep into her skin. The boulevards were crammed with girls of her age, happy, laughing and stylish.

'You've gone rather quiet,' Luc said. 'Don't tell me you're tired.' Following the direction of her eyes, he sagged against the red paintwork of his car. 'You want to go in there, don't you?' he asked wearily.

'There isn't time, is there?' she asked hopefully.

'I'll be over there.' Luc pointed across the square. 'I didn't get to speak to New York this morning. The time change was against me. I'll try now. Join me when you're ready. I'll line up a couple of fruit juices.' He finished cramming everything into the boot and slammed it shut. 'And remember, any more carrier bags will have to stay on your lap. We couldn't fit anything bigger than a pea pod in the boot.'

The doorbell pinged as Rhianna edged into the shop, fighting an attack of nerves. Supposing it was one of those exclusive places that didn't price things, and she didn't have enough money to pay?

'*Bonjour, Madame.*' A pert-faced girl, dressed in an outfit similar to the one displayed in the window, greeted Rhianna. It was too late to back out now Rhianna thought, as she walked forward and pasted a confident smile on her face.

'*Bonjour.*'

'Ah, you are English? 'Ow can I 'elp you?'

'I was looking at your window.'

'You like my display? I do it for the summer. Everyone likes the sea, no? The turquoise stripes I think, with your red 'air and green eyes. Yes?' The brown eyes darted over Rhianna's jeans and T-shirt. 'You must try them on.' She made a noise at the back of her throat as she noticed the fruit stain. 'You 'ave been shopping? And your hair, it is ébouriffé.'

'I, er, is it?' Rhianna got the general meaning of her words. She was a mess. The idea of stripping off didn't seem such a good one now, but before she could think of a suitable objection she was bundled into a small cubicle clutching cropped trousers and two tops.

Even Rhianna didn't recognise the person smiling back at her in the mirror. Cut along elegant classic lines, the T-shirt did all a French T-shirt should do and the trousers somehow emphasised the slimness of her hips, yet did nothing to detract from the femininity of her figure. She drew back the curtain and stepped back into the salon.

'*Magnifique.*' The assistant clapped her hands. 'And you must 'ave these.' She produced a delicate pair of sandals, decorated with large daisies the same colour as the stripes of the top, and a sporty white beret. 'There.'

'You don't think the beret's a bit too much?'

'*Mais non.* It is you.'

Rhianna had to admit she was right. With a straw shoulder bag, the look was complete; cool, elegant, styled. 'You must wear them, now. I will parcel up your old things. You are on holiday?'

'I'm staying in Haut Roque, it's part business, part holiday.'

'Do you know Luc Fermier?'

'Er, yes, I'm staying at The Pavillon.'

The assistant raised a knowing eyebrow. 'That is nice for you.'

'Are you a friend of Luc's too?'

'*Non,* but in St Cécile everyone knows of everyone else.' She chatted, as she filled an enormous bag with the discarded clothes. *Luc is going to have a fit at the size of it,* thought Rhianna as she watched the assistant's nimble fingers at work.

'So while you are 'ere, you will need a dress for the evening.'

'Will I?'

'Of course. I 'ave just the thing. Wait.'

Rhianna was no match for the assistant's very efficient sales technique.

She disappeared into the back of the shop. Rhianna squinted out of the shop window to check the time. The bell on the Hôtel du Ville clock tower chimed half past four. She could see Luc seated at one of the cafés, head bent over his mobile.

'*Voila.*' The assistant returned with a pink sundress made of soft silk.

'I never wear pink.' Rhianna recoiled. 'It doesn't go with my hair.'

'Nonsense. You will wear this,' the girl insisted as she took it off the hanger. 'Look how well it falls and the colour, it changes with your movements. You see? Blue tints?'

Fascinated, Rhianna watched the skirt swirl as the assistant held it against her body.

'Try it on,' she urged. 'For you I do the special deal.'

Rhianna found herself back in the cubicle staring at yet another stranger in the mirror. This time she looked as sophisticated as the girls strolling along the boulevards outside.

'What do you think?' she asked with a nervous smile, drawing back the curtain. It had been such a strange day. Rhianna almost thought she hadn't woken up and the whole thing was a dream.

'*Parfait*. French girls would kill for an English complexion like yours. It is so soft, so smooth, so pale. The sun — pah, it ruins the face. You were wrong about the colour, too. It is marvellous. Monsieur Fermier must take you to dinner when he sees the dress. I will wrap it in tissue paper for you.'

Rhianna refused to look at the amount on her credit card slip. Instead she glanced across the square. Luc was inspecting his watch and then peering in the direction of the boutique.

'*Merci, Madame*.' Rhianna picked up the stylish dress box and the bag containing her jeans.

'That is Monsieur Fermier, is it not? Outside the café opposite?'

'Yes. I think I'd better join him.'

'Such a pity about him and his wife.'

'Thank you again. What?' Rhianna had already opened the door.

'She was an actress, and she preferred to live in America. It was better for her career. I don't think they were very happy together.' She shrugged. 'Come and see me again when you are next in St Cécile,' she added, the businesswoman in her taking over from the gossip. 'I will 'ave new lines in soon. Goodbye,' she called after Rhianna as headed across the square.

5

Rhianna struggled to keep pace with Luc as he strode towards the ticket kiosk. Her new sandals were rubbing sore places on her toes. It had been a mistake to wear them for such a physical outing.

'Not scared of heights, are you?' he asked.

'No.' Her reply was curt and breathless.

The whole retail therapy thing yesterday hadn't seemed such a good idea once she'd got back to The Pavillon. The silk dress, she decided, was totally inappropriate and probably wouldn't ever see the light of day unless she got invited somewhere really swish. *What on earth made me buy it?* she'd thought as she hung it in the back of her cupboard. She ignored the tiny voice in her head suggesting it might have been for Luc Fermier's benefit.

'We could drive to the top of the plateau, but it might make you dizzy. The road's really bendy and it's not easy to pass other vehicles.' Luc turned back and waited patiently while she caught up with him. 'We could also hire bicycles but after that enormous English breakfast, I don't recommend it.'

'You had bacon and eggs too,' Rhianna protested.

'Only one rasher and one egg, and how did you manage hash browns and mushrooms as well?

'I was hungry.'

Rhianna couldn't understand why she'd eaten so much, either. As far as breakfast went she was a piece-of-fruit-or-cereal person, but this morning, the air had felt so active it had sharpened her appetite. The little pavillion lent itself to leisurely breakfasts that lasted well past her usual coffee time.

The countryside was so quiet, Rhianna had overslept again. After a hurried shower, she'd got coffee, eggs and bacon on the go. Luc had been reading paperwork outside, so she'd joined him, and together they'd shared the bacon and eggs, then relaxed with more coffee, fruit juice and croissants, until Luc had suggested an outing to the limestone plateau with its fort museum, pointing out that they couldn't laze around all day doing nothing until Ayshea arrived.

'We'll be unpaid taxi drivers while she's here, I'm sure,' he'd remarked, closing his laptop and briefcase, 'so there will be little time to relax.'

Rhianna was wondering what had gone wrong between Luc and his American wife. Had the marriage been in difficulties when they had first met? Was that why Luc had paid her so much attention, then rebuffed her when he remembered he had a wife?

'Ready? We're going out, aren't we?' Luc interrupted her thoughts.

'Perhaps I ought to see to Ayshea's room?' Rhianna felt honour-bound to offer to prepare it. It was a pretty room, opposite hers, but it needed airing. From what Rhianna could see, Luc's part-time help hadn't been very active with the duster and hadn't even bothered to turn up this morning.

'Ayshea can see to it herself and choose her own colour scheme when she gets here. It'll give her something to do. And you don't want to waste a lovely day indoors, do you?'

'You are sure you don't mind Ayshea joining us?'

'I would have said if it wasn't convenient,' Luc replied patiently. 'Now, if you are ready, come along. We haven't got all day.'

Luc hustled Rhianna to the car before she could change her mind.

★ ★ ★

'You're not wearing your new hat.' Luc held out a hand and yanked her up the final few steps to where a man in a wooden hut was selling cable car tickets. 'You might need it at the top of the plateau. The midday sun's quite powerful up there.'

'I just thought a beret might be a bit overdressed for a day out like this.'

'It suited you.' His eyes moved slowly down her body to the cropped trousers, then back to Rhianna's face. 'I can see Haut Roque is already working its magic on you. You have a healthy colour in your cheeks.'

Rhianna felt her feet slip from under her again. She was severely out of practice at this sort of thing — both the hill-climbing, and also receiving masculine compliments.

'You mean without the stained shirt and jeans, I look almost human?' She tried a light-hearted smile, but wasn't sure she'd pulled it off. Luc carried on looking at her and didn't smile back.

'I mean you have freckles on your nose, you don't look so worried and the sunlight up here dances in your golden hair.'

Rhianna blinked. It wasn't often she was stumped for words. But no one had ever called her hair golden before. The best Sax had come up with was a resemblance to dead autumn leaves.

Her new top stuck to her back. Rhianna would have liked to flap it about a bit to cool down. Her fingers hovered over the neckline but with Luc looking at her so intently, she desisted.

She would be glad when Ayshea arrived. A third person would create a distraction. She knew this sort of banter was routine to Luc Fermier, but Rhianna wasn't on such solid mental ground. Experience had taught her there was no sense in getting light-headed about holding hands with him. It had been a practical move while they'd been climbing the steps. Neither was there any sense in being stupidly starry-eyed because Luc admired her new clothes. Her relationship with Luc, she reminded herself sternly, was purely business, nothing else.

She had fallen victim to his particular brand of charm once, and it was not a mistake she was about to repeat. It was unfortunate that circumstance had thrown the two of them together again at this vulnerable time of her life, but she was up to the challenge.

She straightened her shoulders and as Luc began to search for loose change for the fare, seized the opportunity to release her hand from his and move away.

Rhianna looked down the valley. Luc Fermier was a man of the world. He had time on his hands, while he recovered from a broken marriage. It was masculine psyche to look for a diversion, to prove he was still attractive to the opposite sex, and who better than the silly girl who had made her feelings known after one glass of wine too many? Rhianna still blushed when she remembered his amused tolerance of her attempts at seduction.

Rhianna was now getting over a personal family trauma and the desertion of her fiancé for another woman, but if Luc thought she was still a target for his charms, he was very wrong.

Rhianna was in no mood for romance. The fragile stability of her relationship with Ayshea would take up what remained of her emotional strength. There was nothing left for Luc.

'There's a ten-minute wait.' Luc strolled back to where Rhianna was pretending to admire the scenery. She turned as casually as she could to face him.

'I don't mind. Is that a heat haze in the valley?' She was pleased her voice sounded steady.

'No, morning mist. It should burn off soon. It's going to be warm later. I hope we'll be able to see something when we get to the top of the plateau. The views are magnificent.'

'How long does it take to get up there?'

'About fifteen minutes.'

Luc placed a hand on Rhianna's shoulder. The touch of his fingers, through the cotton material of her top, had the hairs on the back of her neck doing the strangest things. Yet there was nothing suggestive in his movement. He wasn't even looking at her. There was no reason for her to be so jumpy.

'Look, over there,' he pointed, moving his face almost against hers.

'Where?' Rhianna clutched her new bag containing her mobile phone and purse. It was the only barrier she had to keep his body away from hers. The problem was, she didn't know how to use it without looking ridiculous. She felt absurd, straining away from him, when all he was doing was playing the host, pointing out the local sights. She unclenched her hands in an effort to lighten up and tried to concentrate on what Luc was saying. He was hardly likely to behave inappropriately halfway up a hill slope in broad daylight, waiting for a cable car.

'Can you see those straight rows of what look like bushes from here? They're vineyards. Years ago they were owned by the family who had our château built. The family was very influential in the area and at the time of the Hundred Years' War, owned nearly all the land you can see. But with taxes and bad crops they had to sell it off bit by bit, until there was nothing left. Eventually one of the big conglomerates bought them out.'

'That's a shame.'

'What can't be cured must be endured.' Luc sounded philosophical. 'I know you don't drink much wine, but you must try the local vintage. It's a light white, very refreshing. We'll visit the village auberge one evening, have a meal too. It would make a nice night out for Ayshea. We could show her a touch of local colour. What do you think?'

'I'm sure Ayshea would enjoy it,' Rhianna replied, careful not to sound too enthusiastic.

'There's some spa water produced locally as well, but I don't recommend that.' Luc wrinkled his nose. 'It used to be very fashionable at the turn of the century and with clever marketing it's had something of a revival.' He flashed a quick smile at her. 'But it still doesn't stop it tasting disgusting.'

'*Monsieur, 'dame,*' the man from the kiosk called out, '*c'est arrivé.*'

'That's us.' Somehow Rhianna's hand was in Luc's again. His fingers were firm and cool against hers as they strolled across to the entrance where the attendant was waiting for them by a turnstile.

'Have a good day.' The attendant raised his peaked cap as he slid the car door across and waved them on their way.

They were the only two passengers, and Rhianna moved to the far side of the cabin to look out through the large windows to the panoramic views below. They shimmered in the sunlight. The cable wheels groaned into action. With a lurch they began their ascent towards the summit. Soon the cars below them grew smaller as they darted like ants up the mountain roads. There was the occasional flash of colour and Rhianna could just make out a small trail of horses, probably hired from one of the stables Luc had pointed out to her.

Rhianna gripped the handrail and wished she'd brought her camera. The views were stunning. The cable car rose steadily above the mist as the sun broke through the morning cloud. Its rays caught the flame of her hair. She tossed her head back, enjoying the sensation of warmth on her face.

From the other side of the cab, Luc watched her intently. Rhianna O'Neill wasn't a bit as he'd expected. In the years since he'd last seen her, she had changed from a gauche teenager to a stylish woman who knew her mind.

He hadn't been prepared for her beauty. He hadn't been prepared for Ayshea, either. When he'd seen the two sisters together, he'd experienced a spectrum of feelings. He'd wanted to laugh as Rhianna took her younger, yet much taller sister to task and almost marched her over to the telephone, to call and apologise to her headmistress for all the trouble she had caused.

But the situation had been too

serious for amusement. Rhianna had every right to be furious. When she finally looked at him, with eyes the colour of a summer sea, so mad that her hair was almost on fire, he'd almost found himself unable to speak.

He couldn't bear to remember the pain in her eyes when Sax had walked in on the situation and delivered another bombshell.

'What's that noise?' Rhianna looked nervously up at the machinery above them.

Luc dragged his thoughts back to the present. 'At a guess I'd say it's your mobile telephone.'

Rhianna snatched up her bag from where she'd placed it on the floor.

'Steady on.' Luc was by her side in an instant as her comb and purse fell out. He picked them up. 'It's an incoming call, that's all. Probably Jasmine ringing to see how you are.'

'It won't be Jasmine. It's a new phone and I haven't had chance to give her the number, and I've told Ayshea she must only use it in an emergency. She's already in trouble with Miss Adams for making calls to France. Hello?'

Rhianna screwed up her face. The static was so loud Luc could hear if from his side of the cable car.

'You're breaking up.'

'Rhianna?'

'Ayshea? Where are you?'

' . . . station.'

'Where is she?' Luc demanded.

'What?' She flapped her hands at him to be quiet as she tried to make out what Ayshea was saying.

'Accident . . . '

'You've been in an accident?'

'Motorbike, doesn't speak English, French, not good.'

'You're in France? Ayshea, you're not supposed to be here today.'

' . . . early. Can you come?'

'What is it? What's the matter?' Luc hissed, his eyebrows drawn together in an angry frown.

'It's Ayshea.'

'I gathered that much.'

'She's been in an accident.'

Rhianna yelped as Luc snatched the telephone away from her.

'Ayshea. It's Luc.'

The cable car swayed. Rhianna's breakfast churned in her stomach.

'Her French isn't good enough for an emergency. Give the phone back to me,' Rhianna insisted.

'Where are you. Ayshea?' Luc ignored her. 'Tell me and we'll be there as soon as we can.' His voice was firm and in control.

The cable car juddered and ground to a halt. 'We've stopped.' Rhianna dug her fingernails into Luc's arm.

'The mobile signal's gone too. I think she said she was in St Pierre. That's about twenty kilometres away. There's a police station there.'

'What are we going to do?'

'Nothing we can do for the moment.' Luc looked out the window.

'How can you say that?' Rhianna shrieked. 'We're stuck half way up a mountainside. It'll take us another fifteen minutes to get to the top. There's half an hour's wait before we can get down again and Ayshea's been injured. Don't you realise how serious the situation is?'

Luc's fingers encircled her wrists.

'It's all right,' he crooned. 'Take a deep breath.' Mesmerised by the expression in his eyes, she did as he told her. 'Good girl. Now another. There's nothing to be afraid of. The controller will realise we are stranded and soon have us moving again.'

'I'm claustrophobic.' Rhianna's eyelashes were wet with shock as she battled with her fears.

'Everything's fine and Ayshea is safe and well. She may be in trouble, but she's not been hurt.'

The cable car juddered, wobbled then slowly re-started its ascent.

'There, see? We're already on our way.'

'How do you know Ayshea hasn't been hurt?'

'If she was injured she wouldn't have been making the call, would she?' Rhianna scrubbed at her nose with a tissue.

'I didn't mean to panic.' She hiccupped. 'It's just that every time Ayshea telephones, there's a drama. I'm still not convinced she has turned over a new leaf. We had loads of fights at Abercoed. We even had one on the day of our parents' funeral. Then she ran away from school, and now this. It's too much. I can't cope.'

Rhianna didn't see Luc move. The heat of his body enfolding hers was firm, strong, stimulating. Rhianna swayed. She could feel his heart hammering against hers and she wanted to stay in the sanctuary of his arms for always.

'Rhianna,' he murmured into her hair.

'No.' She wrenched herself away. What was she doing? Ayshea was in desperate trouble, and she was in danger of kissing Luc Fermier.

'What's wrong?'

She grasped the handrail in an attempt to support her trembling legs.

'Stay away from me,' she gasped.

'Why? Surely you don't think I was going to attack you. What kind of man do you take me for?' he demanded.

'One who has no scruples about taking advantage of a female trapped in a ski lift. I wouldn't be surprised to learn you'd bribed that official down there to stop the wretched thing.'

'Now you're talking nonsense.' Luc said slowly.

Rhianna's heart was beating so loudly she was amazed Luc couldn't hear it. 'I came on this trip,' she did her best to speak slowly and clearly, 'to get away from Sax and that sort of thing.'

'What sort of thing?'

'Men. Relationships. Call it what you will. Have you forgotten I've lost my fiancé to another woman?' She tossed a stray curl off her face. 'Well, let me tell you, Luc Fermier, I've learned a lot of lessons over the past few years. I may be a lot of things, but I'm not weak, and the sooner you learn that the better.'

The cable car swayed violently as it neared the summit, toppling Rhianna towards Luc, where she landed against his body.

'Now there,' his voice was so close to her ear, his breath made her shiver, 'I do believe you.'

Rhianna sprang away from him. The look in his eyes was driving her senseless. She didn't know what was happening to her. Had she felt like this in her early days with Sax? She wanted to say yes, but her brain was firmly telling her no. She'd never felt like this in her life. The tips of her fingers tingled. She longed to feel Luc's lips against hers, his firm chest crushing the softness of her own body.

The light was sharply cut off from the day, as the car slid into the arrival shed and docked into the landing station.

'In case it has escaped your attention,' there was a teasing note to Luc's voice now, 'we've arrived. And you can't stand there all day looking as though you'd like to do unspeakable things to me. We've got your sister to rescue. Come on. Something tells me we are about to embark on yet another adventure.' He nudged her towards the exit. 'Let's see if we can persuade the operator to schedule us an extra trip.'

On feet that felt like lumps of clay, Rhianna staggered out of the door, onto the landing ramp.

6

The police station was seething with activity. Luc had driven his Aston into the forecourt at breakneck speed and Rhianna jumped out before he'd come to a halt. She hurtled through the swing doors and into reception, ignoring Luc's shout of alarm as he'd been forced to slam on the brakes.

A harassed gendarme was raising his voice to a body of people grouped round the desk. The decibel level was deafening.

'You 'ave to wait.' With much arm gesturing he tried to make himself heard and understood.

'I've been waiting for ages.' One female body leaned forward. 'Why can't I make another call?'

'I 'ave explained. No, mam'zelle. I cannot let you use it.'

He swept the desk telephone out of

her grasp. Several files cascaded onto the floor. He stooped to retrieve them.

'Excuse me. I'm looking for my sister.' Rhianna elbowed her way to the front of the desk and called to the red-faced gendarme. 'Where is she?'

'You speak English?' The gendarme looked up in relief. He staggered to his feet clutching the fallen files.

'Rhianna.' There was a screech and a pair of arms was thrown round her neck. A damp body almost caused her to lose her balance. 'I've been waiting hours.'

'You are this lady's sister?' the gendarme asked in surprise as he deposited his files back on the desk.

The two women hugging each other did not look like sisters to him. One was blonde and beautiful. The other — his eyes lingered on her ravishing red hair. She was very beautiful too, he decided, but her beauty took longer to hit you.

'Yes, I am. I mean, *oui*.'

Flattened against a wall and fighting

for breath Rhianna peered at him around Ayshea and tried to smile. Locked in Ayshea's stranglehold grip, all she could manage was a grimace. She turned her attention back to her sister who was clinging onto her like a limpet.

'What happened?' She worked her hands up and down the back of Ayshea's T-shirt. 'Are you hurt?' Her quick body-search revealed no obvious injury and as Ayshea had hit her with the speed of a torpedo, she deduced her legs were in working order.

'Where've you been?' Ayshea's breath was hot against Rhianna's neck. 'This place is gross. Can you smell the garlic? It's making me feel sick.'

'Ayshea, listen to me. Are you all right?' Her body was hot, too, but Rhianna could feel her shivering.

'Everyone's treating me like a criminal.'

'Have you been arrested? Have they read your rights? Have you called for legal aid?' Rhianna fired questions at her.

'I haven't done anything wrong.'

'Ayshea, I need to know what's going on.'

'They don't understand English.'

Rhianna's shoulder blade cracked against the wall as Ayshea gave her another hug.

'Ease up, Ayshea. I can't breathe.'

Ayshea let go and Rhianna massaged the back of her neck. The palm of her hand was slippery with sweat. She wrinkled her nose, suspecting the smell of garlic might be coming from her. They'd stopped to buy some before their cable car trip and Luc's car reeked of it.

Ayshea's breath was coming in heavy sobs as she tried to explain what had happened.

'Slow down. Now, take your time and tell me exactly what happened.'

'I wasn't sure if I'd got through to you on the right number.' Ayshea was still rushing her words. 'Why'd you change your mobile phone?' Her face threatened to cave in completely. 'It's been awful.'

'What's been going on?'

She felt a draught of air from the swing doors slice through the heavy atmosphere. A shadow crossed the floor towards them.

'Luc?' Ayshea sidled closer to Rhianna who was glad she still had the support of the wall behind her. The expression in Luc's eyes was grim.

'Are you causing more trouble?' he demanded, glaring at Ayshea.

'Can't you see she's in shock?' Rhianna began to get her breath back.

'What happened?' Luc ignored Rhianna. His voice was no warmer than the expression on his face.

Ayshea's blonde hair had turned dark brown with sweat and her bright red cheeks were streaked with dried tears. 'Rhianna?' she pleaded.

'Tell us what happened.' She tried the velvet glove approach. She knew from experience that intimidating Ayshea would not solve any problems.

Ayshea gulped. 'It was all so quick.'

'Where are your friends' parents?'

Luc asked, glancing around. 'We need to speak to them.'

A shifty look of guilt crept into Ayshea's blue eyes.

'They're not here.' Her voice was a whisper.

'Why not? Were they injured in the accident?' Rhianna demanded.

'No.' Tears slipped down Ayshea's face. 'Rhianna, it was horrible.'

'We've done that bit.' Rhianna was growing impatient. 'Look, just tell us what happened. You haven't been arrested, have you? You weren't driving or anything stupid like that?'

All sorts of possibilities crammed into her head. Ayshea was wild, but not that wild — was she?

'*Monsieur?*' Luc unpeeled his eyes from Ayshea as the desk clerk waved a hand at him. '*S'il vous plaît.*'

'Stay here,' Luc instructed, 'don't move so much as a muscle.'

'Luc,' Rhianna protested. 'Ayshea's in shock.'

'This is France. My country. I make

the ground rules here.'

He strolled over to the desk. Rhianna longed to aim a kick at him. Luc glanced over his shoulder, caught the expression on her face and as if reading her mind, acknowledged her expression with the ghost of a smile.

There followed a rapid exchange in French between the two men. Rhianna did her best to follow what they were saying but they were talking too fast. She noticed there were a lot of hand gestures and glances in Ayshea's direction.

Rhianna caught a few hushed words — *accident, motocyclette, hôpital*.

'Motorbike? Did you hit a motorbike, Ayshea? Is that it?'

'No.' Her sister snuffled into her shoulder.

'What then? For heaven's sake, tell me.'

'It was horrible. I was only trying to help. No one else could speak both English and French. I tried to translate but I don't know if anyone understood.

The ambulance took the others to hospital for a check-up.'

'Your friend and her parents are in the hospital?'

'No. I didn't know them.'

'Didn't know who?' Rhianna repeated.

'The police brought me here.' Ayshea didn't answer the question. 'They said I could make a telephone call. Then I was left all alone for ages and I thought you weren't going to turn up. What took you so long?'

'We had no idea you were even in France,' Rhianna retaliated, deciding now was not the time to add she'd happened to be stuck in a cable car half way up a limestone gorge being embraced by Luc Fermier.

She turned her anger on Ayshea. 'Your behaviour's been totally irresponsible. You're old enough to know better. Where are your friends? Surely they speak a smattering of French?'

'This is all your fault.' With a stubborn thrust of her chin, Ayshea hurled her old chestnut at Rhianna, who realised with a sinking heart that their relationship had slipped back into its regular footing.

'It is not!' Rhianna retorted. She watched Ayshea blink in surprise at this refusal to play the underdog. 'Taking the blame for this fiasco is not an option, Ayshea. If I have anything to do with it, you're going straight back home and you can spend the summer gated at Abercoed with Sax and Heidi for company, while you mug up on your grades and get ready to retake your exams.'

'You wouldn't send me back, would you?'

Rhianna fought to harden her heart against the plea in Ayshea's eyes, which were huge with a mixture of fear and shock. She felt ashamed of her outburst. It was easy to forget Ayshea was still only sixteen.

'Can you give me a good reason not to?'

'There was a mix-up with Mr and Mrs Peters' arrangements. They had to delay their departure, a family illness or something. I tried to telephone you from England but I was using your old mobile number and it didn't work. Then there wasn't time to try the new one before we left and I couldn't get a signal on the ferry. Did you have it turned on? I tried lots of times.'

'What do you mean, before we left? Left where? Who is 'we'? And what were you doing on the ferry? Your friend and her parents were bringing their car over on The Shuttle.'

'It was awful. I kept thinking about Mummy and Daddy's accident and driving on the other side of the road. It's so different and everyone drives so fast. I'm so pleased you're here, Rhianna.'

Overcome now with remorse about the way she had shouted at Ayshea, Rhianna hugged her sister. Luc yanked the two of them apart.

'Luc,' Rhianna protested, 'there's no need to be so rough.'

Luc took no notice of her. 'I'll deal

with you when we get back to The Pavillon,' he said to Ayshea as the look of panic returned to her eyes.

'Don't speak to my sister like that, Luc. She's been in an accident.'

'No, she hasn't.'

'And you're being completely — what was that?' Rhianna's neck whiplashed from Luc to Ayshea.

'I was trying to tell you,' Ayshea began.

'Not even the slightest bump, from what I've been told. The female doctor has already looked her over. Isn't that true, Ayshea?'

'Yes.' Her voice was no more than a husky whisper.

'Didn't you know it's a crime to leave the scene of an accident?'

'I didn't leave the scene. I was left there, all alone.'

'Will someone please tell me what is going on?' Rhianna implored.

'This sister of yours,' Luc explained with a killer look at Ayshea, 'decided she didn't want to wait the extra two days to come out with her friend's parents, so when a local lad said he was on his way to France the next day on his motorbike, Ayshea got her roommate to cover for her again. They cooked up some story about meeting up with you in Dover.'

'What?' Rhianna exploded.

'It gets better,' Luc went on. 'Driving like a maniac on his motorbike, this boyfriend gets stopped for speeding.'

'Ayshea? This isn't true, is it?' Rhianna demanded.

'Bits of it are,' she admitted unhappily. 'There really was an accident. A car had gone off the road but it was nothing to do with us.'

'You were swerving to avoid them,' Luc said accusingly.

'No,' Ayshea insisted. 'That bit wasn't true. We got caught for speeding, but as the police stopped us, they saw the other car in the ditch and realised the occupants were in trouble. I tried to help because it was being driven by an English family and they couldn't speak French.'

'At which point her gallant boyfriend seized his opportunity to do a bunk and drove off into the night, leaving Ayshea stranded at the roadside.'

Rhianna collapsed against the wall. Her legs wouldn't support her and she would have slid down to the floor had Luc not sprung to her side.

'Get her other arm, Ayshea.'

'She's a deadweight,' Ayshea complained.

'Do it, now.' Ayshea jumped to obey. 'Help me get her outside.'

'You mean we can leave?' Ayshea gasped her question as she linked Rhianna's arm round her shoulder.

'I can walk,' Rhianna protested.

'You'll both do as you're told,' Luc insisted, 'unless you want to stay here all night.'

'No way am I spending another moment in this place. Come on, Rhianna, get moving.' Ayshea dragged on her arm, anxious to put as much space as possible between herself and the police station. 'We're leaving.'

Rhianna swivelled round. 'They're not pressing charges?'

A wry smile twisted Luc's lips. 'Despite everything, it seems your sister was helpful, sitting with the English family and making sure the children weren't too scared.'

Red in the face, Ayshea mumbled, 'I did what I could.' She glared at Luc. 'It wasn't exactly my fault that my stupid cowardly boyfriend drove off.'

'Some boyfriend,' Luc retaliated, then added, 'Get a move on. We haven't got all night. *Merci, monsieur,*' he called across to the desk clerk who had stopped filling in forms to watch the little procession make their way outside. The look on his face indicated his relief.

The air was cool in the forecourt and Rhianna managed to disentangle herself from Ayshea and Luc and walk unaided, if unsteadily, across the car park. 'I'm sorry. Thought I was going to faint in there.'

'It was very hot,' Luc conceded.

'What's that funny noise?' Ayshea stopped to look around her in alarm.

'Crickets in the undergrowth,' Luc replied. 'Stay here. There's some water in the car. I'll go and fetch it.'

The two girls sank onto a bench and Rhianna closed her eyes again. She felt Ayshea's lips against her hair. 'Sorry, sis,' she murmured. 'I couldn't wait to see you, but as usual it went pear-shaped. I make these wonderful plans, but they always seem to go wrong. I think I'm a bit too impulsive.'

Rhianna's smile came out as a low groan.

'What was that?'

'I said, 'Sometimes you are so like your father'.'

'Am I?'

Rhianna stroked some hair off Ayshea's face. She looked about ten years old now, and the love and trust in her eyes wrung Rhianna's heart.

'Don't worry. I wouldn't have it any other way.'

Ayshea's face was worth every

moment of pain the girl had given her.

Luc was back with a bottle of mineral water. He held it to Rhianna's lips. It was warm and not very pleasant, and tasted faintly of garlic, but Rhianna gulped obediently.

Luc screwed the lid on firmly. 'Get in the back of the car,' he instructed Ayshea. 'Where's the rest of your luggage?'

'I only had a rucksack,' Ayshea mumbled.

'Right then, we're going home, and one more peep out of you and you'll be on the first ferry back to England. Understand?'

'Rhianna's already threatened me with that one,' Ayshea grumbled as she helped Rhianna to stand up.

She missed the softening of Luc's eyes as he watched the two of them stagger to his car. Life with his ex-wife Octavia had never been like this. Sylish, organised and very American, Luc had sometimes wondered if she'd actually possessed a heart.

Rhianna, with her beautiful, hurt eyes and gentle, independent spirit, had too much heart. And as for Ayshea, if he didn't watch out, every able-bodied male in the district would be queuing up at his door to take her out.

When Jasmine had persuaded him to take Rhianna away from Abercoed, he hadn't immediately appreciated that Ayshea would be a part of the deal. He wasn't looking for more life complications. Over the last two years, his life had been horrendous — legal battles, court hearings, arguments over the tiniest detail, until in the end he'd told Octavia to take what she wanted, and headed back to France.

Luc yanked open the passenger door. His threat to send Ayshea back to England seemed to have worked, he noticed with a grim smile as he pushed the seat forward and she climbed in meekly.

'I'll get in the back,' Rhianna offered. 'Ayshea's too tall.'

'Let her suffer. It's her fault that we

are in this mess in the first place.'

'But she'll get cramp.'

'It won't do her any harm. Are you feeling better?' Luc asked Rhianna.

She settled herself into the seat. 'Actually,' she admitted, 'I'm starving.'

'So am I,' a voice joined in from the back of the car.

Rhianna swivelled round in her seat. 'Do you remember those Dublin Bay prawns we had on holiday in Ireland?'

There was a scrabbling noise from the back seat as Ayshea moved forward, smiling now, all thoughts of French prison cells, motorbikes and accidents forgotten.

'That day we got lost and walked for miles? And met the funny man with a donkey cart who couldn't understand a word we said?'

The two girls laughed at the memory.

'We bought some langoustines yesterday in the market,' Rhianna said. 'We've got some French bread at home, too. If we stop off for wine we could have a welcome party for Ayshea, couldn't we, Luc?'

Luc tried to glare at the two pairs of eyes fixed hopefully on his, one girl with hair the colour of an angel's and the other the colour of rusty seaweed. He closed the passenger door and walked round the car. It had been ages since he'd felt such a peculiar sense of anticipation in his stomach.

He roughly reversed the car out of the parking bay. He didn't want to think about anticipation curls. He didn't want to think about Rhianna O'Neill with eyes like the Atlantic Ocean and hair like a mermaid's. She had made the position between them absolutely clear.

'We'll call at the auberge and get some champagne,' he relented, 'to celebrate Ayshea's arrival. Does that suit the pair of you?'

The next moment a pair of young arms was thrown around his shoulders as Ayshea kissed the back of his neck in delight.

Luc's eyes met Rhianna's. With a rueful smile, he turned the steering wheel and headed for home.

7

They all slept late the next morning. After their indulgent supper, the two girls had staggered upstairs, arms round each other, giggling and ducking their heads to avoid low beams.

'You're in here.' Rhianna opened the door. 'I didn't have time to get you new curtains or anything like that, but the shutters will keep out the light for the time being. We'll go shopping next market day and sort things out.'

'It's lovely.' Ayshea walked in and turned round.

'There's not much room, and I haven't made up the bed.' Rhianna tried to follow her in, but there wasn't enough space and they collided in the doorway. 'I'll get some clean sheets and towels for you from the cupboard.'

Ayshea opened her arms. 'What can I say? Thank you. Oh, thank you,

Rhianna.' She hugged her sister and whispered into her ear. Rhianna stiffened and pulled away.

'What was that?'

'I said I think if you and Luc could get together, I'd be so happy.'

'Get together?' Rhianna repeated in shock.

'He's so right for you. Better than that egotistical creep Sax with his headbands and tattoos.'

'Sax was not a creep.' Flames burnt the sides of Rhianna's face. 'You don't know what you're talking about, Ayshea.'

'Yes, I do. I saw the way Luc looked at you over the top of his champagne glass. He's nuts about you.'

'Stop it.' Rhianna glanced over her shoulder. 'I am certainly not in the market for a relationship with anyone.'

'So?' Ayshea raised an eyebrow. 'Don't you like him?'

They'd left Luc downstairs, checking emails, but The Pavillon wasn't very big and Ayshea hadn't bothered to lower her voice. Rhianna did not want him overhearing what she had to say.

'Don't start spreading rumours about me and Luc. There is absolutely nothing between us.'

'It's cool. I won't let on.'

'There's nothing to be cool about, and keep your voice down. It may interest you to know that Luc is getting over a very unpleasant divorce,' she said in a low, firm voice. Ayshea had to be stopped before she went too far. 'He hasn't said much, but I gather he lost his house in America.'

'You mean Luc was married?' Ayshea's eyebrows met her fringe.

'Yes. But if he wants to tell you about it, he'll do so in his own time.'

'Understood. But, hey, that's terrific. If that means he'll stay here and we can spend the summer doing things together.'

'May I remind you the official reason you are here is to improve your French? And the best way to do that is by getting a job.'

'Rhianna,' Ayshea protested, 'give me a break. I need a couple of days to unwind.'

'First thing in the morning.' Rhianna was adamant. 'Now do I get to use the shower before you use up all the hot water?'

Rhianna had not fallen asleep until fingertips of dawn were creeping through the slats of her shutters. Had it been the champagne loosening Ayshea's tongue and making her say those ridiculous things? Had Luc's eyes softened towards Rhianna when he had looked at her, or was it only a trick of the light?

Rhianna wriggled under the sheets. If they hadn't softened, they had definitely looked different in the cosy intimacy of the dining area.

Like the bedrooms, the downstairs rooms were small, and they'd had to squash round the table, joshing elbows, laughing and banging knees as they set to on the langoustines.

The champagne had flowed. Luc had delivered a rather pompous lecture to Ayshea and tried to set a few house rules but, as neither girl had bothered to listen to him, he had given up and joined them in devouring the shellfish and the baguettes dripping with garlic butter before the two girls demolished them all.

The meal had been topped off with fresh local strawberries. It was hardly a romantic dinner, but it had been fun. Luc had been at his most light-hearted and Ayshea, showing no remorse for the trouble she had caused, had talked non-stop about exams and school and what she was planning to do with the summer and how much she intended to enjoy herself. Rhianna was grateful there was no trace of the sulky, bad-tempered girl who'd stormed about the barn at Abercoed.

*   *   *

The next morning Rhianna clambered out of bed feeling as though she hadn't slept a wink. Despite the previous evening's impromptu party, Rhianna knew Luc must regard the pair of them as a nuisance. Two sisters would severely cramp his summer style. He was a highly attractive man and word would soon get round town that he was back and newly single.

Rhianna decided the best course of action would be to get on with the job she'd originally been sent down here to do, and that was to try to arrange Bede's appearance at the Fête du Chanson. Luc had told her the main organiser lived locally. It was time Rhianna had a word with him.

'Good morning.' Luc was pouring coffee as Rhianna emerged on to the sun terrace. 'Want some?'

'Yes please.'

She watched the sun creep up the grass. Why did the weather have to be so beautiful?

'No sign of our guest?' Luc asked, the coffee pot hovering over a second cup.

'Ayshea's still asleep. I looked in on my way down.'

'Leave her where she is, then.' He put the pot down. 'Things will be chaotic enough when she wakes up.'

Rhianna sat as far away from Luc as possible under a sunshade, but it wasn't shady enough to hide the dark circles under her eyes.

'You look pale,' he remarked. 'Didn't you sleep well?'

'Not very,' she admitted.

'You probably ate too many langoustines. They can be a bit rich. It was quite a night, wasn't it? Let's hope Ayshea will settle down and not cause any more trouble.'

'I wouldn't put money on it.'

'Then I hope we're available to pick up the pieces. I forgot to mention that the gendarme was actually quite impressed with the way she handled herself after the accident.'

'Don't tell her.' Rhianna took a croissant. It was warm and soft. There was a fresh, buttery smell as she broke it open. 'Let her think she's in disgrace. Believe me, life will be a whole lot easier.'

'Here, try some of this strawberry

jam. There are jars of it in the cupboard. By the way I've asked for regular local help with cleaning and cooking, now there are three of us here.' He leaned back in his wicker chair with a frown of concern. 'Are you sure you're feeling well?'

'I'm fine,' Rhianna snapped back at him.

Luc raised his eyebrows. 'Something's wrong, isn't it?'

Rhianna wished she hadn't sounded quite so terse. She was no good at confrontation.

'No — of course not.'

'Why the frosty treatment then?'

Rhianna put down her knife. 'Luc,' she began. 'I think we ought to get one or two things straight.'

'Yes?'

'Firstly, Ayshea gets a job.'

'I'll go along with that. What else?'

'I need to get on with making arrangements for Bede's performance at the Fête du Chanson.'

'The mayor's your man. Haut Roque

is not big enough to have one so we share with St Cécile. I'll drive you over. We'll visit him this morning. It will make up for our disrupted outing yesterday.'

'I prefer to go on my own.'

Rhianna watched the smile evaporate on Luc's face.

'You want to go without me?' he repeated, as if he hadn't understood what she'd said. 'Why?'

Rhianna was aware of the birds singing their hearts out, the smell of moist grass being warmed by the sun, the deep brown hurt of Luc's eyes as her message got through to him.

'I'm not ready for — ' she floundered as she searched for the right word.

'Something I wasn't offering,' he clipped back, his eyes growing cold.

'No. You don't understand. I need time to sort out where I want to go with my life. I don't want to repeat my mistakes.'

'I don't want to hear about your hang-ups.' Luc's chair scraped the flagstones as he stood up. 'I'll leave you to finish your breakfast on your own. Let me know when you want to leave and I'll give you the directions.'

Rhianna watched him stride indoors. She hadn't meant it to be like this. She'd wanted to explain how the wounds Sax had inflicted were still raw and hadn't fully healed. Luc's embrace in the cable car and last night's supper had brought back the memories of her early days with Sax, when they had been young and carefree. She couldn't go through all that again. She'd wanted to explain. But Luc hadn't given her a chance.

And there was no simply walking out on him, as she'd done with Sax. Ayshea needed stability in her life. They couldn't go rushing back to Abercoed on a whim. Sax and Heidi wanted time alone together and there was no room for extra trauma in an already tangled personal situation.

Why had Rhianna taken Ayshea's nonsense seriously? The girl's words had been the product of an over-active imagination and too much excitement for one day. Rhianna had been guilty of misreading Luc's behaviour, and now she'd conjured up the sort of situation she'd been trying so hard to avoid.

She watched the fragrant strawberry jam drip off her knife, making a deep red pool on her plate.

Her relationship with Ayshea was beginning to resemble that of proper sisters now, talking and laughing and sharing secrets. Rhianna wanted to keep it that way. But where did that leave her relationship with Luc? Life could get complicated, living under the same roof.

She couldn't leave Ayshea here on her own with Luc. That wouldn't be right. And if things went according to plan, Jasmine and Bede would be coming over soon from Italy, expecting her to have arranged things locally for them. She had no choice. She'd have to stay on at The Pavillon.

A shadow danced along the patio and

disturbed her thoughts.

'Luc's a grump this morning.' Ayshea, all long brown arms and legs in cream top and shorts, emerged from the double doors. 'Have you had a lovers' tiff?'

'Of course we haven't.'

Rhianna coated her croissant with a generous helping of strawberry jam and bit into it. She couldn't engage in conversation with Rhianna with her mouth full, but the knowing expression in Ayshea's eyes left no doubt as to her take on the situation.

* * *

'*Non, mademoiselle.*' The mayor was adamant as he spoke to Rhianna. 'We do not have the facilities.'

'Surely you could make an exception?'

'A singer of Monsieur Evans' class would attract many extra visitors. Where would they park? They need to eat, accommodation. Non.' He repeated more firmly. 'It is a local event, not an international gala.'

'Mr Evans wouldn't want to take over, or anything like that,' Rhianna insisted. 'And if we didn't announce his appearance until perhaps a day or two in advance, there wouldn't be that many extra people.'

'Why then does he want to appear?' the mayor asked, perplexed.

'He loves singing. He loves France. He wants to help boost your charity appeal.'

'That is all very admirable, Mademoiselle O'Neill, but my duty is to the citizens of the area. I cannot agree. And now I have a very busy schedule today.' He shook her hand. 'Goodbye.'

Finding herself dismissed and standing in the village square, Rhianna looked round in disappointment. Now what was she going to do?

She couldn't believe the mayor had actually said no. To sing at the local fete would give Bede so much pleasure, and the villagers too. She was sure of that. Bede loved to stay in touch at grassroots level. Despite his international reputation, he was a philanthropist at heart. He'd throw himself into the event with his customary enthusiasm and give as much of himself as he gave at the great opera houses, but he wouldn't play the big star.

And but for the pigheadedness of one man, he would have happily appeared at the local Fete du Chanson.

Rhianna bit her lip. Luc would know whom to approach next, but she couldn't ask him. After breakfast he had handed over written directions to St Cécile without a word. Rhianna had begun a halting apology but his mobile had started to ring, effectively cutting her off, and Luc had turned his back to take the call.

Outside the mayor's office she unchained the daily help's bicycle, which she'd borrowed, not wanting to bother Luc for the car keys.

The hedgerows were alive with summer as she wobbled along the country lanes from St Cécile. The little bridge spanning the river was bumpy but solid. Rhianna looked down into the meandering water below as it twisted its way along. Small fish darted backwards and forwards, sunlight glinting on their orange backs.

Glancing at her watch, she hitched herself back onto her saddle and rode on past tenant cottages, fields full of poppies and cheerful tourists in bright T-shirts. Horse-riding children waved at her and hot-looking ramblers trudged along, leading a loaded donkey in their wake.

She didn't immediately notice a bicycle similar to her own travelling with equal speed from the opposite direction. With a bump and whirl of revolving spokes they collided, both riders falling off in a tangle of arms and legs.

'Ah, it is you.' The annoyance on the girl's face changed to a beaming smile. 'Yvette — you remember me, of the dress shop in St Cécile? I am so sorry. I was not looking where I was going. The donkey, I was admiring its panniers.'

Rhianna shook herself down. 'It was my fault too. I hope you aren't hurt.'

'I am used to falling off. I am so nosey. I do not look where I am going.'

'Have you time for a coffee?' Rhianna suggested.

'No. I regret I do not. I must work on a day like this, my day off. It is a pity, but until I meet my millionaire I cannot afford to give up work.' She smiled. 'I am still looking for 'im. They are not thick on the ground, and the sale, it starts next week. I really could do with some assistance.'

'My sister is over from England for a few weeks,' Rhianna offered eagerly. 'She needs to practise her French. She's only sixteen but she's willing to learn. Would you like her to help?'

'Excellent.' Yvette beamed. 'Tell 'er to come as soon as possible. I am sure she will be perfect.' Yvette heaved herself back onto her saddle. 'I will look out some bargains for you both. Last year's fashions, but I give you a very good price.'

Yvette wobbled on her way, and with

a lighter heart, Rhianna climbed back onto her own bike. At least one problem was sorted. She looked down at her oily legs and grimaced. Bicycle chains were no respecters of stylish trousers. The turn-ups were smeared in grease. Yvette, on the other hand had looked cool and collected in her cotton print top and shorts.

★   ★   ★

By the time Rhianna had cycled back to The Pavillon she was hot and thirsty. The cool air along the tree-lined drive was a welcome contrast to the sun, and Rhianna paused only to wash her hands and face in the stone sink before going in search of a drink.

'What have you been doing?' Ayshea demanded from the terrace. 'You look hot and your pants are filthy.' Her nose wrinkled. 'Is that oil? It smells.'

Too late Rhianna realised Ayshea was not alone. Luc was working at one of the wooden benches. He stood up and bowed courteously, but there was no welcoming smile in his eyes.

'I fell off the bike. Glad you find it so amusing,' she retaliated.

'Hey, sis, lighten up.' Ayshea spread her arms. 'It's a lovely day. What were you doing bike riding around the country-side?'

'I went to St Cécile.'

'Did you have any luck with the mayor?' Luc broke in.

Rhianna wished now she'd taken the time to change her top and comb her hair, but she'd been unable to resist the jug of iced lime juice placed on the kitchen table and she had poured herself a glass before strolling out onto the terrace.

'No.' A combination of sun and the expression on Luc's face scorched her skin. She longed to dive into a cold shower. 'He said he thought Bede would try and take over and as it was a local thing it wouldn't be appropriate.'

'Bede's not like that,' Ayshea objected.

'He said Bede would draw in the crowds.'

'That's what they want, isn't it?' Ayshea butted in again.

'The demand on local facilities would be too heavy.'

'Where do they normally hold the Fête?' Ayshea asked.

'We take turns,' Luc replied. 'This year it's ours here at Haut Roque.'

'Couldn't you override this local bigwig? Tell him you won't stage the Fête here at Haut Roque if he doesn't let Bede sing?'

'It's not for me to say. I'm not even on the committee, but they will have a problem this year, with or without Bede's contribution.'

'Why?' Rhianna demanded.

She'd been leaving Ayshea to ask all the questions, but underneath her silence she was seething. Why hadn't Luc told her all this before she'd made a fool of herself with the mayor? She ignored the voice in her head telling her she hadn't hung around long enough, but pedalled off before Luc had finished his telephone call.

'We used to use the grounds of the chateau when it was privately owned and for several years we carried on with the arrangement, but now the conglomerate have refused permission for us to use them this year. It's a management thing, I think. They did say they were committed to the community, but it doesn't look like it includes classical festivals.'

'Stink bombs,' Ayshea exploded, 'if that isn't the pits.'

Her outrage drew reluctant smiles to both Luc's and Rhianna's lips.

'I think it's more a case of local politics. It was probably why the mayor didn't go out of his way to help. He wants the festival to be held in St Cécile every year. It's a big event. All the houses are decorated and people wear their regional costumes. There's a procession and sometimes film crews come down and record it. It helps tourism in the area. Naturally, he wants all the glory to go to St Cécile.'

'It looks like Jasmine will have to make

other arrangements for their summer break,' Rhianna said with a sigh.

'You can't give up like that without a fight, Rhianna.' Ayshea looked outraged. 'You owe Jasmine, big time.'

'What do you suggest I do?' Rhianna retaliated.

'I don't know, but you've always been a fighter. You can't roll over and let that twerp of a mayor walk all over you.'

Rhianna smiled reluctantly at Ayshea and ran a hand through hair that felt like tyre ribbons.

'I've run out of ideas,' she admitted. 'If we were at home things would be different, but we're guests here and it doesn't do to break the rules.'

'You'll come up with something,' Ayshea declared. 'You always do.'

Ayshea's confidence in her was due for a nasty knock, Rhianna thought as she sucked a piece of fresh lime dry before waving the rind at Ayshea.

'Forgot to tell you, I've got you a job.'

'What?' Ayshea protested. 'But I want to sunbathe.'

'Not all summer, you don't. Besides, too much sun is bad for your skin.'

Ayshea's glare matched Luc's as she looked at Rhianna.

'It's in a boutique in St Cécile. You can go over in the morning. You'll like Yvette. She's expecting you, and she needs some help.'

Ayshea stood up. 'In that case, I'm going to get the sun lounger out now before you sentence me to hard labour.'

She stalked off towards the garden shed. Two sets of eyes followed her progress down the patch of grass towards the wooden hut. A few moments later there was the sound of banging and a few choice words of basic Anglo Saxon coming from inside.

'I should really help her,' Luc didn't sound too enthusiastic as he leaned back in his chair, 'but I'm waiting for New York to call.'

'I'm going to take a shower.' Rhianna sniffed. 'I'm not sure, but I think that smell is me.'

'Don't go.' Luc put out a hand and

trapped hers under his. 'I want to talk. About us.'

Rhianna's throat dried again and she wished she hadn't finished her glass of juice. Her eyes were drawn to his suntanned arm and the soft light brown hair that looked as gentle as thistle-down, an odd contrast to the very masculine muscles it protected.

'Not now. Ayshea might hear us.'

'So what if she does?'

'Can't it wait?'

'No.' Luc tightened his grip on her hand. Rhianna cast an agonised look at Ayshea who was emerging backwards from the shed. Any moment now she'd turn round.

'Was it because of what happened in the cable car yesterday?' he demanded.

'What are you talking about?'

'Your coldness and defensiveness this morning, at breakfast time?'

Ayshea, who'd finally won her battle with the sun lounger, cast a triumphant smile in their direction, then caught sight of Luc's hand on Rhianna's. With exaggerated discretion and a wink at Rhianna she looked away, seemingly intent on sorting out the framework and erection technique of the ancient piece of garden furniture.

'Because I'm not sorry I did it. And neither, I think, are you. Is that what's bothering you?'

'You're not being fair.' Rhianna leaned forward and immediately wished she hadn't. Luc put out his other hand and touched her hair. Over his shoulder she could see Ayshea grinning, capering round the sun lounger and making a thumbs-up sign behind Luc's back.

'How about if I promise to respect your personal space?'

If Rhianna hadn't been sitting down she'd have collapsed. Everything about Luc, his voice, his eyes, his mouth, was driving her senseless. How could she be feeling like this when a few weeks ago she had thought Sax was the love of her life?

The dull ache behind Rhianna's eyes made thinking difficult. The sun was too hot for her complexion. She wanted to go indoors and bathe her forehead with lavender, then lie down until the raging heat coursing through her body had subsided.

'What say we have dinner together tonight down at the auberge, without your sister?'

'I don't think that is a good idea.'

'And start over as friends?'

'No.' She turned her head away.

'Lovers, then?'

'Stop it,' Rhianna implored, not sure if Luc was teasing her. His eyes had softened and Rhianna found herself wishing he would go back to being angry with her. 'Ayshea . . . ' she began.

'Judging from the gestures she'd making behind my back, I think she'd be delighted if we were a couple.'

'What gestures?'

'All that prancing around on the lawn. The mirror.' Luc did his quirky smile and pointed towards the house. 'In the dining room. I can see her reflection. She's now pretending, very badly, to sunbathe.'

Rhianna followed the direction of his eyes. Ayshea was holding a magazine upside down and evidently trying not to crow.

'There's my call.' Luc dropped Rhianna's hand as his phone began to ring. 'Eight o'clock tonight? I promise to behave like the perfect English gentleman.'

8

The following week passed in a flurry of activity. Ayshea had telephoned from St Cécile one morning, soon after she had starting working for Yvette, to demand, 'Have you spoken to Jasmine and given her the bad news about the Fête?'

Rhianna had been hovering by the telephone, wondering how she was going to pluck up the courage to make her call.

'I was just about to,' she confessed.

She'd tried the mayor again, with her biggest smile and best French, hoping maybe she'd caught him on a bad day, but he'd been equally adamant. The answer was still no, unless she could assure him that adequate facilities would be available. It was pointless trying to approach the other committee members, Luc had informed her. The mayor held the casting vote.

Rhianna hated to admit it, but it looked like defeat. There was nothing to keep her here any longer. She'd have to return to Abercoed and see if she could sort out alternative arrangements for Bede and Jasmine's late summer break. But how was she going to break the news to her wilful half-sister? It would be a severe step backwards. Ayshea was settling in so well and had already made several local friends.

And where did that leave her relationship with Luc? Questions crammed into her brain and she didn't have the answers to any of them.

'Don't do anything until you speak to Yvette.' Ayshea's voice down the telephone was high with excitement. 'I'll pass her over.'

'Rhianna? Ayshea tells me you have problems with the Fête?'

'Yes — the mayor won't agree to it.'

'He is an old fool, that one, he is full of his own self-importance.'

'I just can't get him to change his mind about Bede and, as we can't use the grounds surrounding the chateau either, we're going to have to abandon our plans unfortunately.'

'I can assist.'

'You can? How?'

'Remember my millionaire?' Yvette laughed down the line. 'When we collide on the bridge? I mention to you?'

'I remember you saying you were looking for one.'

'Well, I have found 'im.'

'What?' Rhianna gasped, wondering briefly if Luc was Yvette's new man friend. She ignored the searing stab of jealousy coursing through her veins as she tried to breathe normally.

'I 'ave made a good friend who works for the conglomerate at the chateau. He is in an important position.' Yvette paused significantly.

'Congratulations,' Rhianna said weakly, feeling foolish about her suspicion regarding Yvette and Luc.

'If I speak to my friend I am sure 'e will agree to let us use the gardens. It will be so beautiful and I know the local people will want to hear Monsieur Evans perform. He is a fine singer.'

'Yvette?' The significance of her words began to sink in. 'Could you? Really?' Rhianna now felt a surge of excitement.

'Leave it to me. You go ahead and make your plans.'

Jasmine had been overjoyed when Rhianna had finally got through to her in Italy and told her the news.

'That's wonderful news, Rhianna. Bede is finding this tour very tiring. He is such a perfectionist. I'm going to insist he doesn't take on so much in future. But you know what he's like. He doesn't like to disappoint people and he loves to sing. The break in France will be exactly what he needs to wind down afterwards.'

'Then I'll go ahead and arrange things this end, shall I?'

Jasmine softened her voice. 'I've missed you, Rhianna.'

'I've missed you too, Jasmine.'

Rhianna thought longingly of the cool waters and gentle peace of Abercoed. But all she could see in her mind's eye was Luc Fermier's face. She couldn't deny her feelings any longer. True to his word, he had kept their relationship strictly platonic and as the days progressed, Rhianna hardly thought of Sax any more. She was in danger of falling in love with Luc Fermier for the second time in her life.

'And how are you?' Jasmine asked.

'I'm fine,' Rhianna replied, a shade too quickly.

Jasmine was never fooled by a fib.

'My poor girl. Are you still upset over Sax?'

'No.' Rhianna shook her head firmly. These days, if she thought of him at all, it was with affection — nothing else.

'And Ayshea has arrived safely?'

'Yes, she's here.' Rhianna had decided against telling Jasmine of Ayshea's escapades, it would only worry her.

'Has she settled down?'

'Very well. She has a temporary

summer job, so everything's fine.'

'And Luc Fermier?'

'What about him?' Rhianna kept her voice deliberately casual.

'You know he is a very attractive man.'

Rhianna doodled mermaids on the telephone pad to keep her hands occupied and wished Jasmine would change the subject. She had tried to reset her relationship with Luc on a less intense basis but as the days passed, she knew it wasn't working. And the fault was on her side, not Luc's. Since Ayshea's arrival there were no more intimate dinners, or local trips together. That part of Rhianna's strategy had been successful. Luc often went out first thing in the morning and did not return until late at night. He was polite and pleasant to her and Ayshea, but nothing more.

Rhianna was at a loss to understand how the situation had developed. Luc was different in every way from Sax in looks, temperament and lifestyle.

Rhianna now realised she would always be grateful to Sax. At the time she had thought he had broken her heart but, she realised now, it hadn't been his to break. They had drifted into a relationship that wasn't ready to be developed into something more serious. Rhianna would tell Sax that, the next time she saw him. She truly wished Sax and Heidi happiness and hoped the three of them would always remain friends.

Her pencil worked faster as she coloured in the scales on the mermaid's tail. It concentrated her mind and stopped her thinking about Luc. When had she realised she loved him? There hadn't been one special moment. It had crept up on her, when she wasn't looking.

'It isn't Luc Fermier who is making you sound so relaxed and happy?'

'It isn't anybody.' Rhianna hoped her reply to Jasmine's question sounded convincing. 'The weather's lovely down here and so is the scenery. It's just a relaxing place to be.'

'So my suspicions are misplaced?'

Rhianna was saved the trouble of replying by sudden, dramatic background noises.

'I have to go, darling. Bede is bellowing for me.'

'I can hear him.'

'See you very soon. Bede sends his love. We knew that you wouldn't let us down.'

Rhianna replaced the receiver and dropped her pencil onto the pad. She needed fresh air. She would walk down to the chateau and check it out.

The path was winding and long, but under the trees the air was fresh. It smelt newly washed with lime. Luc had told her that, in season, truffles could be found growing among the roots of lime trees. She couldn't understand how something so unattractive could be such a delicacy.

The pigs are welcome to snuffle them out, she thought as she took deep breaths, enjoying the relief from the sunshine, which was growing steadily hotter day by day.

After about a quarter of an hour and when she was beginning to think she would never reach the chateau, she turned a corner and let out a gasp of surprise. Nothing had prepared her for its beauty.

Renaissance magnificent and golden in the midday sun, with casement windows, round towers, square towers, one tower even boasting an extension of sorts with another little tower growing out of its side. Wings had been added throughout the centuries, creating a glorious hotchpotch of elegance and style.

A tiny drawbridge led over a moat to gardens which, to Rhianna's delight, hadn't been formalised, but left to grow wild. A profusion of poppies covered the grassy front lawns, the air smelt of honeysuckle and bees droned gently, seeking pollen in the large golden hollyhocks growing against the sun-baked walls of the old kitchen gardens.

A corporate flag flapped from yet another tower, the only blot on the landscape, and Rhianna knew from experience that they would have to allow sponsorship to be acknowledged in all the paperwork. Otherwise, the setting was perfect.

Cars could park down the long drive. There was plenty of space to sit and picnic and enjoy the gardens, and the chateau would provide a magical backdrop to the classical concert. There was no way the mayor of St Cécile could raise any more objections.

And due to Yvette's tireless efforts, he hadn't been able to. Her corporate connection had come up trumps and full facilities had been offered to the village, including rooms inside the chateau for the performers to freshen up and change, and accommodation for Bede and Jasmine during their stay.

Ayshea, too, had worked her socks off. Half the local male population under the age of thirty had been captivated by her blonde beauty and, with a face that was no longer sad or sulky, she was able to charm dragoons of men into fetching, carrying and doing the million and one chores the occasion demanded.

After a full day's work at the boutique, she'd often stayed up until midnight, helping out with a group of young friends. Rhianna hadn't enquired too closely as to what they were doing so late at night, but Luc had remarked with a wry smile that her knowledge of the French language had improved enormously.

Allowing herself a few moments out to enjoy the ambience, Rhianna realised with a jolt of surprise that the Fête was less than ten days away. Ayshea and her team really had worked wonders.

★ ★ ★

'Isn't it brilliant?' Ayshea sat next to Rhianna on one of the benches her admirers had cheerfully dragged onto the upper lawn for her exclusive use. 'I can't believe we've got it all together, and so quickly.'

It was the night of the concert and the chateau was bathed in the velvet mid-evening twilight. Fairy lights strung from the trees by the army of Ayshea's admirers swayed brightly in the cool breeze.

'I don't know what to say.' Rhianna looked down to the lawn buzzing with activity and excitement. 'We couldn't have done it without your help.'

The news of Bede Evans' guest appearance had spread, and cars were backing up the drive and overflowing into the emergency car parks. The charity collection boxes were brimming and local volunteers dressed in traditional long shirts with embroidered lace shawls had been delighted with their success.

The village procession had set off from the church in the afternoon and with laughter, song and dance, made their way good-naturedly through the village to the chateau, led by the newly elected Queen of the Fête.

Expectations were running high. Even the inhabitants of St Cécile had been forced to concede the success of the day.

In an earlier ceremony, the keys of Haut Roque had been passed over to Yvette's gentleman friend and the celebrations had started earlier than planned with an impromptu display of local dancing, the men wearing their traditional velvet jerkins and hats bowing ceremoniously to their equally beautifully dressed ladies.

Yvette had been in her element playing lady of the manor, reducing Rhianna and Ayshea to giggles, and in one regrettable incident they'd been forced to hide behind an oak tree while they gave vent to their laughter. They hadn't wanted to hurt their new friend's feelings, but the sight of her regally waving from a horse-drawn carriage was more than either of them could take with a straight face.

'I've never seen anything like it,'

Rhianna admitted.

'And I've never seen anything like your dress, Rhianna.'

Ayshea was wearing one of Yvette's younger models in turquoise, a plain shift with a flat neckline and matching bolero jacket. She looked stunning. In contrast Rhianna had chosen to wear the dress she had bought from Yvette when she had first arrived in Haut Roque.

'You don't think it's over the top?' The silk changed colours in the twilight as Rhianna ran her hands over its sheen.

'I did when I saw it hanging up in your room. I mean, I thought — like yuk, pink silk and red hair? But on you it is something else, Rhianna. I've never seen you look so beautiful.'

Rhianna raised her eyebrows at Ayshea. But her sister was serious. There was no teasing light in the blue eyes, only admiration and love. 'And you know me.' Ayshea's eyes softened to laughter. 'Always told you the truth, didn't I? Even when I thought you were being a pain?'

'Oh yes, you certainly told the truth,' Rhianna acknowledged.

Their relationship had come a long way since the beginning of the year. Rhianna no longer felt so straight-laced and Ayshea had blossomed into one of the nicest people she knew. Guy and Lesley, Rhianna thought with a lump in her throat, would have been so proud of their beautiful daughter.

'I love the way it changes colour.'

Rhianna stood up and twirled for Ayshea's benefit. At that moment a shadow moved out the darkness. Rhianna stifled a shriek and Ayshea spun round to see what had startled her.

'Hello!' She leapt up. 'Wow, don't you look great.' With a laugh she flung herself at Luc and planted a kiss on his cheek.

For one moment the two of them were suspended in time. Rhianna held her breath. The young blonde girl on the brink of life, with her arms round the neck of the darker, older man, dressed in a dinner jacket and smiling down at her, with a familiar expression of amused tolerance.

Ayshea unlaced her fingers from Luc's neck.

'I can't stay here all night kissing you, Luc Fermier,' she joked, 'I've a million things to do.' With a wicked glint in her eyes, she added, 'Rhianna can take my place.'

Before Rhianna could reply, Ayshea was no more than a turquoise dart disappearing in the direction of a knot of young men.

'Doesn't she ever give up?' Luc demanded as he ambled towards her.

Rhianna's eyes drank in the masculinity of his movements. The exploding lights in her head had nothing to do with the lanterns on the trees, or the fireworks arranged for later. They had everything to do with Luc Fermier. He looked magnificent. She sank back onto the bench. Luc sat beside her.

When she didn't speak, he added by way of explanation, 'Ayshea's still trying to matchmake and we all know very well where we stand on that matter, don't we?'

'Sorry?' Rhianna had difficulty clearing her throat.

'Forget it.' Luc shrugged. 'Although I have to admit that dress is giving me ideas.'

'What sort of ideas?'

'The sort Ayshea would approve of.'

Rhianna wanted to move away from him, but she couldn't. She tried to convince herself it was because the bench was of rough wood and would snag her dress. But it wasn't true. She didn't move because she didn't want to. She wanted Luc Fermier to kiss her.

She made a little noise at the back of her throat and closed her eyes. The pressure of Luc's thigh against hers told her he'd moved towards her. There was a smell of lemon aftershave and then the touch of his lips on hers, gentle at first, then hard, then demanding. Rhianna had to cling onto his body, otherwise she would have slid off the bench.

She didn't care if Ayshea could see her from the trees. She didn't care that chattering villagers settling themselves down to enjoy the concert surrounded them. She only wanted Luc to go on kissing her forever.

Finally his lips released hers.

'I'm a liar.' His voice was hoarse against her hair. Rhianna stiffened. 'It's got nothing to do with the dress. Although it played its part,' he admitted. 'I have wanted to kiss you for ages, but you have been so stiff and so English. I messed up my chances with you once, I didn't want to do it again.'

Rhianna blinked. She knew she was being unladylike, but she really wished he'd kiss her again.

'Twice,' she said slowly, 'and I told you, I'm half Irish.' Underneath the silk Rhianna's body was burning.

'And is that the bit that is on fire right now?' His lips touched her ear.

'Luc?'

'What?'

'I'm sorry.'

'Why?'

'I wanted to cool our relationship because . . . '

'There's no need to explain. I understand. Ayshea made things worse, didn't she? Always trying to throw us together.'

'Sax played a part in it too but it goes back further than that. When I first found out you were married — ' Rhianna began, then shrugged. 'I blamed you for my behaviour.'

'I was attracted to you, I admit,' Luc explained. 'At the time Octavia and I were going through a difficult phase in our marriage but she was still my wife, so I was to blame too. But let's not talk about the past.'

Strange shapes and shadows in the trees disturbed the night air around them as they sank into silence.

'You know,' Luc smiled, 'when I saw you and Ayshea together I named the pair of you the firework and the firebrand. You looked so amusing tearing into poor Ayshea, I think in that moment I truly fell in love with you.'

'*Monsieur Fermier*,' a voice called out.

'Do you think whoever it is who wants me will go away if I don't reply?'

'It's the mayor,' Rhianna replied, 'and he's coming this way.'

Luc swore roundly under his breath. 'I hope your French wasn't up to that,' he said before plastering a smile on his face. '*Monsieur?*'

'There is a problem.'

'Wait for me?' Luc murmured. 'We've got some unfinished business. If you're over your love affair with Sax, that is?'

'I think I was over him the moment you stepped back into my life.'

Under the eyes of the local dignitaries, Luc cupped her chin with his fingers and delivered a lingering kiss before standing up to acknowledge the mayor's request.

'Coming,' he called, sensing the mayor's impatience.

Rhianna was glad she had the protection of Luc's back to shield her from curious village eyes while she composed herself. Her hair was rumpled, and her lips felt newly kissed. She ignored the indulgent smiles and approval of the villagers seated round her.

The fountains had been lit up now and in the darkness, the droplets of water sparkled like ice diamonds. Rhianna took a few moments out to watch them. She knew she should be helping the organisers with last-minute emergencies, but her body wouldn't respond to her brain.

'Darling. There you are.' Jasmine's perfume wafted across the night air. 'Bede's in the chateau changing, so I've escaped for a breather. Haven't you been a clever girl, arranging all this for us?' Her delicate features turned from delight to surprise. 'I hardly recognise you. You look as if you are in love.' Her face softened into a picture of happiness. 'I was right, wasn't I? It is Luc Fermier, isn't it?'

'I don't know,' Rhianna confessed. 'He was here a few moments ago.'

'That's why I hid behind those bushes,' Jasmine confessed. 'I saw him being very French.' She laughed. 'There's no need to blush. I'm so happy for you. I can't stay long. Bede needs me. I'm supposed to be looking for a cuff link, but I had to come and say hello. I've got a surprise for you.'

There was a movement behind Jasmine and a second later she was dwarfed by a tall figure in sweatbands, lizard T-shirt and skin-tight jeans.

'Hi, Babes.'

'Sax is going to do a modern number for us. And now Bede will smell a rat if I don't go back.' Jasmine blew a kiss at them. 'We'll catch up with everything after the concert.'

Sax?' Rhianna greeted him.

He ambled towards her, a hesitant smile on his face, hands raised in a gesture of submission. 'If you want to kill me, go right ahead.'

His smile was all she remembered — warm and loving, the smile of a good friend.

'It's good to see you.' She opened her arms.

'You're not mad at me?' he asked in surprise.

'No, Sax. I'm not. Truly.'

'That's wonderful. Heidi's, like, something else. I wanted to tell you I really love her.'

'You don't have to explain. I understand. Where is she?' Rhianna glanced past his shoulder.

'Looking after things in Abercoed. She's a bit tired and didn't feel like making the journey.' Sax put his arms round her and hugged her. 'For old time's sake,' he said, and lowered his lips to hers.

Rhianna kissed him back gently. As she drew away, she heard a sound behind his shoulder. She gasped. Luc Fermier's eyes glittered into the night. He reminded Rhianna of an angry tiger.

'I apologise for disturbing you,' he said coldly.

Before Rhianna could respond, he turned and disappeared into the trees. Ayshea, who'd been standing by his side, stared at her with horrified eyes. Her face, too, was white with shock.

9

'Did I mess up your life again?' Sax called after Rhianna as she ran into the darkness, apologising as she bumped into the crowds coming in the opposite direction.

She heard heavy breathing as Sax, blundering through the undergrowth, caught up with her.

'Babes, like I'm sorry. It was only a friendship thing. Do you want me to explain things?'

'No, Sax, you'll be needed on stage.' She pushed him away.

'Are you sure? I mean, that shape that looked like a bear with a sore head was Luc lurking in the bushes, wasn't it? Heard you and he were an item. Cool.'

His blue eyes danced. *Typical Sax,* thought Rhianna. *He would find the situation amusing.*

'You go back. They're waiting for you on stage. We'll catch up later.'

'Okay, if you say so.'

'Break a leg,' she called after him.

Sax gave her a peace salute and ambled off towards the lawns. Rhianna watched him go with amused exasperation. How could she have thought herself in love with Sax? He was a good friend now, one she would always remember with affection, but that was all. But where did that leave her relationship with Luc? If he didn't trust her with Sax, then what hope was there for them?

'*Mademoiselle?*' A woman in local costume appeared in front of her. 'You are the English lady staying with Monsieur Fermier?'

'Yes.'

'This is for you.'

A grubby piece of paper was thrust at her.

'Where did you get this?' she demanded.

Her question was met with a smiling

shrug and Rhianna realised she'd asked the question in English. She tried calling after the woman in French, but the good-natured crowd had carried her on her way. Rhianna unscrewed the message, which had been squashed into a tight ball, and held it up to one of the fairy lights dangling from a nearby tree.

Got the bike back. Meet me by the lake as we'd planned, when everyone's at the concert, and we'll take off. Love and kisses.

It was unsigned and scrawled in pencil. Rhianna frowned. What bike? The lake? Then she turned the message over and saw Ayshea's name printed on the other side.

Rhianna collapsed against a tree trunk, glad of its solid support. The note wasn't meant for her. It was meant for Ayshea. Ayshea's motorbiker was back. The one who'd given her a lift, then dumped her by the roadside after the accident and driven off into the night.

They were going to run away

together. Thank goodness the message had been delivered to Rhianna by mistake. Thoughts of Sax and Luc fled from her head. She had to get to the lake and stop Ayshea. In the distance she heard the opening music of the concert. She didn't have much time.

'*Monsieur?*' She grabbed the jacket of a man dressed in traditional Limousin costume. 'The lake?'

Her French had now totally deserted her, but the man smiled back and in heavily accented English pointed her to the far side of the wood.

'The other side of the trees, Madame.'

The crowds grew less congested as Rhianna struggled against the flow. In the distance she could hear music and clapping. She had to get to Ayshea before she did something stupid. She couldn't bear to remember the pain in Ayshea's eyes when the girl had seen her kissing Sax. Running away again probably hadn't been an option until then. But now the wild child was back.

Rhianna couldn't let Ayshea give up

everything for an oily biker who, when the chips were down, had abandoned her alone in a foreign country.

She pushed on, not sure where she was going. She would not think about Luc. Ayshea was her priority now.

Besides, Luc would never believe any explanation she offered. It was obvious he still believed her to be in love with Sax, a married man, soon to be a father. That said it all. If he thought she would stoop that low, then they had no future together — despite all his fine words and passionate kisses.

Rhianna lost precious minutes going round in circles until the trees began to thin out into a clearing. In the distance a large lake shimmered under the moon. She sensed movement. Some-one, a man, was standing by the water's edge.

'Hey, you,' Rhianna shouted as she ran down the grassy slope, her silk dress billowing around her legs. The shadowy shape turned towards her. 'I want a word with you. If you think you're making off with my sister, you're wrong. She's only sixteen and I'm her guardian. What sort of creature are you, anyway? Driving off, leaving her alone in the middle of nowhere?' Rhianna was fully charged now and vented all her anger on the silhouetted figure. 'I'll drag you through every court in the land if you try anything. And when I've finished with you, Monsieur Fermier will also do it all to you over again. He's a force to be reckoned with. So don't even think about it.'

She finished with a shriek of surprise as she collided with an all-too-familiar male form. 'Luc? What are you doing here?'

'What on earth is going on?' There was lazy amusement in his eyes as he looked down at her. 'Why are you screaming like a banshee yet again? And what was that you said about me being a force to be reckoned with?'

'Where is he?' Rhianna panted.

'Who?'

'Her boyfriend.'

'There's no one else here. Whose boyfriend?'

'Ayshea's.'

'What?'

Rhianna thrust the message at him. 'Read that. I'll see if they're hiding from us. We've got to stop them, Luc. He can't take her away.'

Luc's loud laughter cutting into the night silenced her.

'The cunning little imp.'

'What's so funny?'

Luc's French accent was very pronounced. 'There is no motorbiker.'

'Yes, there is, and she's going to run away with him. You don't know her like I do. We've got to stop her.'

Rhianna fell over her feet as Luc grabbed her, his strong arms pulling her upright. He swung her round to face him. For the second time she collided with his chest.

'Let me go.' She raised her hands and thumped them vainly against the solid muscle.

'We have some unfinished business of

our own,' he said in a voice that no longer held any trace of amusement.

Rhianna struggled urgently to free herself but Luc's fingers were iron grips on her arms.

'I've got to find Ayshea.'

'We'll deal with her later. Believe me, she's in no trouble.'

'Have you taken leave of your senses?'

'Ayshea is with Jasmine watching the concert. I've just left her dancing to saxophone music on the lawn. Does that satisfy you?'

A raspy breath hurt Rhianna's chest and her nose felt suspiciously wet. She wanted to draw the back of her hand across her nostrils but Luc's eyes, even in darkness, were hypnotising her to stone.

'You're not lying, are you?'

'I've never lied to you, Rhianna.' He put his arms round her back and held her tightly. 'But we're wasting time. What I want to know is, did Sax kiss you like this?'

He sank his lips onto hers and drew

her feet from her shoes as he lifted her body up to his. Rhianna was forced to cling to him as the lake changed position with the night sky.

After what seemed about an hour Luc released her.

'Well?' he demanded, eyes glittering like a lynx.

'No,' she whispered, not sure if her face had turned upside down like the lake. It certainly felt most peculiar. 'It was nothing like that.'

The lake swung back to its proper position. 'Thought so,' he said grimly, before releasing his hold on her body.

She fell back onto her shoes and, losing her balance again, was forced to grab his arm.

'We weren't doing anything,' Rhianna began.

'It looked as if you were kissing each other to me. You call that nothing?'

'As friends, Luc, that's all. Sax was pleased I was happy for him and Heidi, and I was pleased he was happy.'

'And you expect me to believe all that

happy, pleased nonsense?'

'I don't give a fig whether you do or not.' Rhianna tossed her head, spiked with outrage. 'Like you, I don't lie. And if we haven't come here to rescue Ayshea, then I'm leaving. There's nothing else for me here.'

'Oh no, you don't.' Luc dragged her back to him. 'You're not going anywhere until we've had this out. Did you really mean what you said about you and Sax?'

In the distance Bede's voice broke into the night. Its purity always had the power to move Rhianna to tears. Angry in case Luc thought she was crying for him, she dashed them away with the back of her hand.

'I don't know what I said.' Her voice was tight with emotion. 'But you'd better listen, because it's the only time I'm going to say it.'

Luc was still as stone. Something plopped gently into the water. Bede's aria carried across the evening air. Rhianna could think of no better scenario for her own swan song.

'I love you, Luc Fermier, properly this time, not the silly misplaced crush of an adolescent girl.' She heard his feet move on the grass. 'I thought I loved Sax. I was wrong. I also thought, after Sax, I'd never love again. I was wrong about that, too. In fact I haven't been right about a single thing, have I? Now if you'll let me go, I've got to find Ayshea and reassure myself that she really is all right.'

'Ayshea can look after herself.'

'Her boyfriend's waiting for her somewhere. We've got to find him.'

'She set us up.'

'I got her message by mistake.'

'You think so? Then let me put you right. She told me you and Sax were planning to leave together tonight because he'd discovered his marriage had been a big mistake and that you were still in love. She told me if I was quick, I'd catch you both down by the lake. That she'd overheard you planning to leave during the concert. Like a fool, I believed her too. I came down here to confront the pair of you.'

'Ayshea did what?' Rhianna's voice rose in outraged disbelief.

'Exactly. Personally, I think she gets her vivid imagination from you. Perhaps she's kissed the Blarney Stone.'

'She's not Irish. I am.'

'Half Irish,' Luc reminded her gently. 'And now,' his voice was a purr in the darkness, 'that was quite some speech you made about loving me.'

Rhianna longed to dash into the lake to cool herself off.

'I think I'd better go now.'

'You've had your say. It's time I had mine.'

'I don't want to hear it, whatever it is.' Rhianna couldn't stand the humiliation. She could tell by his eyes he was about to let her down. She couldn't take another rejection.

'Will you shut up and listen to me?'

'It's all right, Luc. You don't have to pretty it up.'

'You are the most beautiful girl I've ever met.'

Rhianna stopped struggling. He couldn't mean a word of it, but it was wonderful to hear him say so.

'Even if you can't resist an argument. You're funny, brave, loyal, outrageous and a fighter.'

'I am?' Rhianna blinked. 'When did I have time to be all that?'

'Ever since the day I met up with you again. That's why I was so jealous when I caught you kissing Sax. I wanted to knock his head off. Don't you realise I'm mad about you?'

Rhianna swayed.

'But you don't go for ditzy redheads who doodle mermaids on telephone pads and who have emotional baggage attached to them in the shape of an adolescent half-sister who is always getting into scrapes.'

'Everyone's allowed a few flaws.'

'Did you say you were jealous of Sax?'

'A Frenchman hates to admit it.' The

tiny corner quirk in Luc's smile was reassuringly familiar. 'But yes, I was. You haven't been out of my mind for a second. I wanted to tell you how I felt that day in the cable car, but I realise now it was too soon. Your wounds were still fresh. Then there was Ayshea to consider, then the festival. It was one thing after another. I was nearly going, what's the English expression, up the wall? Seeing you with Sax tonight was the final straw. You don't still love him, do you?'

'What I feel for him now is friendship, nothing more.'

'I wouldn't blame him if he did still love you. You're so easy to love, Rhianna. Everyone loves you. Jasmine and Bede — and Ayshea.'

'She didn't to begin with, and even now we have our bad days. And I expect we'll have a few more in the future.'

'I admit she's given you a bumpy ride but you haven't quit, have you?'

'I wanted to. Lots of times.'

'Not the same thing.' Luc shook his head.

'Luc.' Rhianna was struck by a frightening thought.

'What?'

'Ayshea's part of the deal — if we have one.'

'You're not serious?' he asked, a look of mock alarm on his face. 'You mean I have to inherit a hot-headed half-sister if I want you?'

'The situation's not negotiable.' Rhianna drew away from him.

By now a light mist was rolling off the lake as the temperature dropped in the night air. Rhianna shivered.

'Luc?' she prompted when he said nothing.

'Rhianna?'

'You . . . ' she began again, then bit her lip as her courage and Irish blarney deserted her. How could she ask Luc what she had to know before she made up her mind?

'I what?'

'Do you love me?' she plunged in.

'Mm.' He put his head to one side. 'Think so.'

'Because if you don't, I would rather you told me now.' She blinked. 'Was that a yes?' she asked hesitantly.

'Of course I love you, my darling. Haven't I been trying to tell you for the last half hour?'

'Really? Really and truly?'

'I really and truly love you. Does that satisfy you? I want us to get married as soon as possible and provide a proper home for Ayshea, a stable family background here in France. That's why I've been out for days on end, sorting things out with Octavia's legal people. For a while I thought she might want possession of The Pavillon, but she's happy now in her new relationship and like me, wants to move forward with her life.'

'I can't.' Rhianna shook her head.

'Now what can't you do?'

'Stay in France. I have my job in Wales.'

'Would you mind very much if

someone else did your job in Wales?'

'Who?'

'Heidi, Sax's wife. Jasmine asked me tonight if I'd talk to you about it. You see, Sax wants to live in Abercoed now he's about to be a father. There really isn't enough room for all of you at the barn, and Heidi has settled in well, apart from a few clashes with Bede. And from what I can make out, at some time or other everyone clashes with Bede.'

'You've been discussing me with Jasmine behind my back?' Rhianna drew back from Luc.

'Only to ask if she'd object if I took you away from her. She was upset over what happened with Sax and wants you to be happy, Rhianna. We all do. And I have a job for you here, with me. I've sold up in The States. I'm going to work from Paris and Haut Roque. But I need someone to help me.'

He gestured into the dark. 'To hell with the job. We can sort all that out later. Say you'll marry me? We'll move back to Wales. I'll go down on bended knee. Anything. Rhianna, I can't live without you.'

The lips weren't quirky now as Luc stared down at her. There was no smile on his face. Only the look of a man who was desperately unsure whether he would get the answer he wanted.

'Yes, I'll marry you,' Rhianna said simply.

Bede's voice soared above the night in the final notes of his aria. After a moment's silence as the crowd recovered from the heart-stopping experience, there was an explosion in the sky — purple, gold, green and scarlet stars shot into the air, cascading down in a shower of sparks.

'Would you look at that?' Luc pointed to the night sky.

Rhianna leaned against his body. His heart thumped into her back. 'Remember how I compared you to a Catherine Wheel?' he murmured. 'All spitty and sparky?'

'I think we can expect a few more

fireworks along the way.'

'I don't doubt it.'

'Luc?'

'Don't interrupt. I like kissing your ear.'

'Do we have to tell the others just yet?' Rhianna asked.

'Don't you want to?'

'In good time, but I have to be in the right mood to cope with Ayshea leaping about and taking all the credit for getting us together. And right now,' her lips touched Luc's ear, 'I can think of something better to do.'

'So can I.' Luc's voice was husky with desire. The next moment his lips bruised hers and he slipped a spaghetti strap of pink silk off her shoulder.

Golden stars exploded above them in the night sky before cascading to the ground.